T0063426

The Trial Of Hang Tuah The Great

A Play In Nine Scenes

GHULAM-SARWAR YOUSOF

PARTRIDGE
A Penguin Random House Company

To order additional copies of this book, contact
Toll Free 800 101 2657 (Singapore)
Toll Free 1 800 81 7340 (Malaysia)
orders.singapore@partridgepublishing.com

www.partridgepublishing.com/singapore

CONTENTS

Settings

The scenes of this play are set in 15th century Melaka, 15th century Inderapura, and modern-day Kuala Lumpur.

A Note on Staging

The play should be produced in the round.

Suggested Costume Designs

In general, the costume designs for the various scenes should conform to the styles of the periods in which they are based. It is suggested that for maximum impact, the three judges in particular should be dressed in traditional theatre costumes: Judge 1 in costumes resembling those of Malay royalty, but with a red mask as in *mek mulong* or *menora*; Judge 2 in Chinese opera costumes, with painted face or a mask, and Judge 3 in a *kathakali* costume, with a mask and a traditional headgear.

In the opening scene, Hang Tuah should be dressed in flamboyant modern jacket and pants, such as that worn by a superstar like Michael Jackson, with several medals as well as dark glasses. In later scene(s), he should be dressed in traditional Malay style or in modern western clothes, in keeping with the respective setting and scene involved.

Court ladies and other characters should also be dressed in costumes in keeping with the period and setting of particular scenes—traditional or modern.

List of Characters

Hang Tuah
Hang Jebat
Tun Teja
Dang Wangi
Judge 1
Judge 2
Judge 3
Announcer
Bailiff
George Tan
Felicia
Lena, Datuk Hang Tuah's Secretary
Rahim Long
Man 1
Man 2
Man 3
Woman
Dang Rakna
Susi
Santi
Court Lady 1
Court Lady 2
Princess of Gunung Ledang
Court Officials
Female Attendants

SCENE 1

Kuala Lumpur, 1969. A statue of Hang Tuah, the ancient Melaka warrior and hero, in a public park.

The cyclorama or acting area is brightly lit up. Lights, fireworks, firecrackers, and other noises indicate an atmosphere of gaiety.

SCENE 2

A spotlight picks up the announcer as he enters. His face is painted white, and he wields a staff, also white, in the fashion of a sceptre or baton. Otherwise he is completely covered in black.

ANNOUNCER: Ladies and gentlemen, that was a celebration. It seems a hero has awakened after slumberous centuries. Welcome to this theatre, the abode of dreams. And speaking of dreams, remember they too are important, like living reality, perhaps even more so, though coming from a different dimension.

By the way, allow me to introduce myself. I am, as some of you will know, Awang, the story-teller, though tonight I look a little . . . different.

All the same, I am not merely a face and a . . . staff. To be sure, I am those, but even more so, I am a voice. I wear two hats. One makes me your guide into the glorious past, the persistent present, and the yet unfulfilled future. The other transforms me into a bailiff, for tonight, this place is no ordinary theatre—it is a court house, even a history book, a microcosm of the world. In it, momentous events will transpire, perhaps not earth-shaking, but significant enough nevertheless. You see, our hero, Hang Tuah the Great, is to be tried for certain crimes allowed to pass unexamined for centuries, others nearer to us in time, and still others yet to transpire. Thus, I will become the magic wand to speed you back and forth in time. And if, by the end of two hours, some of the brain cells in this theatre are for the first time given life, or reactivated from a dull slumber, no matter how briefly, my purpose would have been served, the present endeavour altogether worthwhile.

And now, ladies and gentlemen, I am to take you under my wing, fly you to public places where there is excitement over an ancient heroic tale. I can already see impatient performers waiting to emerge into the limelight. So, for now, let this face and staff make way, honourable friends, to three voices from amongst your midst.

The spotlight on the announcer goes off and he exits. The scene changes to a public park. Enter two men and a woman dressed in everyday clothes. The first man is middle-aged while his companion is somewhat younger. The woman can be of any age.

MAN 1:   The fires have given way to fireworks. There is a new spirit everywhere. I can feel it in my bones. This place will never be the same again. Today, after centuries of sleep, Hang Tuah is awake once more.

MAN 2:   What did he look like in real life, I wonder? Was he big sized or small? Was he tall or short?

MAN 1:   Does it matter? Does shape or size matter? Perhaps he's different to everybody who thinks of him. To me, he's shapeless, like the spirits, like the wind. He's everywhere; he's immortal. It's only the foolish who believe he died. Doesn't *Hikayat Hang Tuah* tell us he did not die?

MAN 2:   Just went into the cave of Puteri Gunung Ledang and never returned, I know. I was just wondering. After all, he *was* human, wasn't he?

WOMAN: Yes; but the *hikayat*—surely you don't take it literally? There are errors in it, as any historian or scholar can tell you. Do you know that Tuan Puteri Candrakirana was already dead a hundred years before Sultan Mahmud ruled Melaka? Yet she appears in the *hikayat*. It seems he even married her.

MAN 1:   Is it always necessary to take everything literally? Why don't you think of them as symbols?

WOMAN: Symbols? Can symbols be real?

MAN 1:   Symbols are the most real of things.

MAN 2:   And so all those immortal ones—Galuh
              Candrakirana, Hang Tuah, Ratu Lara Kidul,
              Puteri Sa'adong, Puteri Gunung Ledang—are
              no more than mere symbols. Is that what you
              mean? Didn't any of them really live? I mean eat
              and sleep, grow up, get married, have children,
              and most important, die? They all seem to have
              simply vanished into thin air. Yet they return
              every now and then to intrigue us, haunt us.

MAN 1:   Isn't that what makes life interesting, gives
              continuity to existence? And faith, faith in such
              things is what keeps the world going, makes it so
              beautiful.

WOMAN: I suppose you are right. Life could be dull
              otherwise. Fairy tales and legends of heroes,
              whether in books or on the *bangsawan* stage,
              make life less boring, even tolerable. But to
              believe that they, or at least some of them, are
              immortal, I mean really living and likely to
              appear in our midst like some mist or whiff
              of perfume—that's something else. Even the
              furthest limit of the imagination cannot conceive
              that Hang Tuah, the great warrior and hero, has
              appeared amongst us in person today.

MAN 1:   He has always been around. Only asleep or
              in hibernation, one might say. Now he has
              awakened again. You may call it his second
              manifestation, if you wish.

MAN 2:   You mean just like Vishnu? Many say he will
              be here soon in the form of *Kalki*, his final
              incarnation, since the dark ages, *Kaliyuga*, is
              already upon us. Others, more skeptical, regard

4

the whole thing as a mere myth; I mean the reincarnation idea. One doesn't know what to believe these days. Anything is possible.

MAN 1:   Just let your imagination wander a little; become an innocent child once again, and everything will be pregnant with the potential of truth. Every grain of dry sand, every blue drop of ocean will become a living reality.

MAN 2:   And now that the arrival of *Kalki* is imminent, the end of the world must also be near.

MAN 1:   Who knows? That too may be true. One thing, however, is certain. Now that Hang Tuah has been restored to his rightful place . . .

WOMAN: In the lake gardens near the National Monument . . .

MAN 1:   This country and its people are never going to be the same again.

MAN 2:   The *hikayat* mentions he will return to claim Taming Sari. I believe the time has come.

WOMAN: And where is Taming Sari, if I may ask?

MAN 1:   Taming Sari, like Hang Tuah is a symbol, my friend. It is everywhere and yet nowhere.

MAN 2:   The mouldy statue, it was lying in some *kampung* for centuries. Then it found a place in the Melaka Museum, and now it stands proud in Kuala Lumpur, the federal capital, cleaned, glimmering, a fit monument for a hero.

MAN 1:   Not just a statue, my friend. This whole country is going to be a monument to him. He is its true founder.

WOMAN: Come, come. Surely you are not rewriting Malaysian history? What about Tunku Abdul Rahman, then, Bapak Malaysia?

MAN 1:   Tunku Abdul Rahman is Bapak Malaysia, but Hang Tuah is Malaysia's grandfather.

MAN 2:   And Parameswara, Mat Kilau, and others fit somewhere in between, I suppose—grand uncles and so on. We are indeed fond of heroes.

MAN 1:   Every race, every nation needs its heroes—symbols to which they can turn to re-orientate themselves. They provide the guiding light in dark times when everything turns topsy turvy.

MAN 2:   Perhaps you are right.

MAN 1:   From time to time they return, bearing new names, but in effect not changing at all; only adapting to new times, and circumstances. It's the spirit that endures; the superficial trappings are temporary. Millions like you and I have come and gone unrecognized. Few are remembered—the true heroes.

WOMAN: And, don't forget, the true villains.

Lights dim and fade out. The three persons exit.

SCENE 3

The announcer enters and a spotlight picks up his face. The words he says are boldly displayed on a sign-board.

ANNOUNCER: Kuala Lumpur, 2020 or thereabouts. Hang Tuah is charged in the Sasaran Court with several serious crimes, including the seduction and kidnapping of Tun Teja, the murder of Hang Jebat, the murder of J.W.W. Birch, the 1969 riots, and the failure of the New Economic Policy. He pleads not guilty, and a trial date is set.

The Sasaran Court. The three judges and other officials led in by the announcer as Bailiff, enter to a dignified dance tempo. Following a processional circuit of the acting area, they take their places on three swivel chairs. They are dressed in dignified robes, and the judges faces, frozen, should hold a mixture of expressions. It is suggested that masks be used.

BAILIFF: *Bangun!*

All, including audience, stand. The judges and court officials enter and take their places.

JUDGE 1: Sit down, please. Don't stand on ceremony. After all we are in all of this together (*All sit*). Fellow judges and friends, let me explain the reason for our presence here today in this year . . . (*Looks*

	up at the sign) 2020 or thereabouts. It doesn't matter, the exact year, I mean. It is some time in the future.
JUDGE 2:	And the events in which you are about to participate lie both in the past and the future. This whole thing is, what shall I say, futuristic.
JUDGE 3:	Futuristic. Hmm . . . I like that.
JUDGE 1:	Our first business will be to involve some of you actively in these important futuristic events with some historical basis. And so, let me see (*points out)* you, you, you and . . .
JUDGE 2:	Why not everyone, just to save time?
JUDGE 3:	A marvellous idea, and fully democratic too.
JUDGE 1:	Well then, everyone present in this theatre as an audience member is hereby appointed a member of the jury. We on this bench are the interrogators, the inquisitors, if you like. And yes, the note-takers, the recorders, members of the press, and so on.

As they are introduced the court personnel by turn bow or show some other sign of acknowledgment to the audience.

JUDGE 2:	Do you all accept the appointment to serve as members of the jury in this historically important futuristic trial of the hero of ancient and modern times, Hang Tuah the Great?
	Some commotion, doubt and uncertainty among the audience.

8

JUDGE 3:   Why don't we assume they accept? After all we know their minds.

JUDGE 2:   Fine, just to speed up things a little. I take it you all accept the universal nomination.

JUDGE 1:   Now, bring the accused in.

A dramatic clash of cymbals, and then some jazzy music— kompang, Chinese cymbals, trumpets, nadhaswaram, anything. Hang Tuah is brought in procession, seated on a sedan chair like a Maharaja or superstar with several dancing or pompom girls. He is immaculately dressed in a suit, with medals all over his chest. He wears dark glasses. The audience cheers, whistles, throws flowers, etc. It is an entry befitting a hero. He responds to the cheers, waves to the audience, sends flying kisses at the ladies. Upon arrival at the dock, Hang Tuah stands in it. Other participants in the procession disperse. Silence.

JUDGE 1:   Please take your oath.

H.TUAH: I swear to tell the truth, nothing but the truth, and nothing but what I believe and imagine to be the truth.

JUDGE 2:   Give us your full name, please.

H.TUAH: Hang Tuah Ibni Al-Marhum Hang Mahmud; Tun Tuah; Laksmana Tuah; Hero of Malacca; Giant Killer of Sayong; Maharaja Lela; Mat Kilau; Hero of 1969; Hero of the Malay Race . . .

JUDGE 3:   All of those!

H.TUAH: Yes, Your Honour, and yet others too; they can actually fill an A4 sheet, typed single-space. My

9

names and titles—they have changed from time to time, from circumstance to circumstance.

JUDGE 1: Perhaps, but they are too long, far too long. Can you cut the non-essential ones out, so that they can fit into our computers?

H.TUAH: Your Honour, they are all essential facets of my identity. It is near impossible to remove any of them. But I will try, for the sake of your computers. Yang Berhormat Laksmana Hang Tuah Ibni Almarhum Hang Mahmud. How about that?

JUDGE 3: Still too long.

H.TUAH: (*Exasperated*) Still too long? Your Honour, everything recorded here today will belong to posterity. In keeping with my status, my dignity, my place in history . . .

JUDGE 2: We understand, we understand, but . . . the computer system . . .

JUDGE 1: What's on your identity card?

H.TUAH: I have no identity card, Your Honour.

JUDGE 2: No identity card? How is that possible?

H.TUAH: I just never got one, Your Honour. In those early days in Bentan where I was born, they had not yet invented birth certificates or identity cards. The same was the case in Melaka when I lived there. All we needed was a password. Identity cards, birth certificates, citizenship papers, and other such documents were later colonial inventions, to keep track of us so-called natives; and when I got famous . . . well, there was no need . . .

JUDGE 1:   Let us not waste time. Just tell us how we should address you in this court.

H.TUAH: Laksmana Hang Tuah Ibni Almarhum Hang Mahmud. How about that?

JUDGE 2:   Too long.

H.TUAH: (*Remains silent for a while*) Just Hang Tuah then: short and sweet.

JUDGE 1:   That's excellent, very precise. What is your age?

H.TUAH: I don't know.

JUDGE 3:   Don't know? How is that possible?

H.TUAH: You see, Your Honour, I was born in Bentan during the reign of . . . Sorry I can't remember the name of the ruler. I then migrated to Melaka during the reign of Sultan Mansur Shah whose dates are not precisely defined. According to Richard Winstedt, it was sometime in the 15th century that Sultan Mansur Shah ruled the port-town of Melaka, and this being the year 2019 or thereabouts, that makes me between 550 and 600 years old. But my exact age does not matter, Your Honour. I am still going strong.

JUDGE 3:   How in the world is that possible?

JUDGE 1:	In those ancient days, anything was possible, my friends. You see the Bible tells us Adam lived to the age of 930. Noah lived for 950 years, and Methuselah, he lived the longest of them all; I don't remember how many years exactly, but Bernard Shaw confirmed it.
H.TUAH:	Nine hundred and sixty-nine, Your Honour.
JUDGE 1:	Thank you. Any relative of yours, by the way?
H.TUAH:	Only a distant one, Your Honour, through Adam.
JUDGE 1:	Place his age down as approximately 600 years. Occupation?
H.TUAH:	Over the years, I have had many distinguished careers Your Honour, I was a body guard, warrior, *laksmana*, businessman, banker, politician, minister, and playboy, *inter alia*.
JUDGE 2:	What's your present occupation?
H.TUAH:	Nothing in particular, Your Honour. I sit on my laurels.
JUDGE 1:	Put down "Unemployed". Well, now that we have finished with the preliminaries. Let's get down to business. Read the charges, bailiff.
BAILIFF:	(*Bowing*) Yes, Your Honour. (*Reads as previously*).
JUDGE 3:	One last bit of detail before we proceed. What is our race?

H.TUAH: Race, Your Honour?

JUDGE 3:   Yes, race . . . *bangsa.*

H.TUAH: Oh, I see Your Honour. My race is *bangsa* Melayu.

JUDGE 2:   Is that what is says in your identity card? Oh, I am sorry, I forgot; you have no I/C card. Actually, there have been stories circulating that you are of Chinese origin, of the Hang clan, like many others who came to Melaka during its early days, including Hang Li-Po.

H.TUAH: Not true. Not true, Your Honour. I have also heard that some think I am Orang Asli, Chindian, Indonesian, Bangla. Actually, I am beyond all races, yet I belong to them all. My ancestors never for an instant worried about these things, Your Honour. For the sake of convenience, my *bangsa* I said to be Melayu. I have no real problem with that.

JUDGE 1:   Now that the preliminaries have been settled, Hang Tuah, how do you plead to the charges as displayed on the placard, and as read by the bailiff?

H.TUAH: Your Honour, distinguished members of the jury, I plead not guilty.

JUDGE 2:   Do you therefore seek a trial?

H.TUAH: No, Your Honour. No such thing. I seek honourable discharge.

JUDGE 3:   That's impossible. The charges are serious and still stand. There has to be a trial.

H.TUAH: Then so be it, Your Honour. Even though I am a great hero, I see that I have no say in these matters. Since destiny has obviously decreed that I be tried, let it be so. If you remember, the Persian poet Omar Khayyam, in Edward Fitzgerald's famous translation of his *rubaiyat,* says with such elegance:

> The moving finger writes and having writ
> Moves on; nor all thy piety nor wit
> Shall lure it back to cancel half a line,
> Nor all thy tears wash a word of it.

So, what can I do but go along with the learned and oft-quoted Khayyam?

JUDGE 2:   Will you require a lawyer appointed by the Legal Aid Bureau?

H.TUAH: No, no, Your Honour. I prefer to keep my destiny in my own hands. Thank you.

JUDGE 1:   Fine. It appears you are fairly learned, quoting Omar Khayyam and all that.

H.TUAH: Thank you for the compliment, Your Honour. In my time, I learned a dozen languages, I believe, and a little bit of this and that besides. I could also recite some *ayat* of the Holy Quran from the last chapter. In those dark times, I was one of the most highly literate; Your Honour. It's a pity there were no universities then, or I would have collected a string of degrees, real as well as

14

honorary ones. And yes, Your Honour Omar Khayyam happens to be one of my favourite poets.

JUDGE 1:   Brother judges, note-takers, recorders, members of the Jury. Since Hang Tuah has pleaded not guilty, a trial will take place at a date to be fixed by the court, hopefully in the very near future. There is bound to be great public interest in this case, locally and perhaps in neighbouring lands and beyond. Remember, as my distinguished colleague here mentioned, this whole event is futuristic, but it is also historical and current. I suggest that between now and the time we next meet in these august chambers, you do some homework. Perhaps you can read Kassim Ahmad's *Hang Tuah*, published by Dewan Bahasa dan Pustaka in 1964. There are also several excellent plays on the theme, including Usman Awang's *Jebat*. To get yourself acquainted with matters germane to this trial, you may find Tunku Abdul Rahman's *May 13th: Before and After* useful and, of course, do not forget Mahathir Mohamad's controversial *Malay Dilemma*. The newspapers and other documents in the National Archives should also prove interesting. All this will help refresh your memories. For those of you who are too lazy to read, or unfortunately illiterate, the principal events will be re-enacted in this theatre, right before your very eyes. Be wary, however, for every director has his own viewpoint with which you may or may not entirely agree. Owing to the very serious nature of the charges the accused will not be allowed bail. He will remain in custody in case he decides on further adventures in Bentan, Melaka, Inderapura or elsewhere. This court now stands adjourned.

OFFICIAL: *Bangun!*

Music. All including audience stand. The judges and officials exit, followed by Hang Tuah. Lights fade out.

SCENE 4

The announcer enters, with the spotlight only on his face. The words he reads are also displayed on the signboard.

ANNOUNCER: Hang Tuah is charged with the seduction and kidnapping of Tun Teja, and of having illegally entered Inderapura, as Pahang was known then, with the intention of effecting the same. He pleads not guilty, and the trial begins. (*Exit*)

The Court-house as before. Hang Tuah is in the witness stand. Music, the judges enter and take their seats with other officials.

JUDGE 1: Bailiff, please read the charges.

BAILIFF: Yes, Your Honour. Hang Tuah, you are hereby charged with the seduction and kidnapping of Tun Teja, and of having illegally entered Inderapura, as Pahang was then known, with the intention of effecting the same.

JUDGE 1: How do you plead, Hang Tuah?

H.TUAH: I do not deny the charges, Your Honour.

JUDGE 2: Does that mean you are now pleading guilty?

H.TUAH: No, Your Honour. I am not guilty.

JUDGE 1:	Did you or did you not kidnap Tun Teja?
H.TUAH:	I did kidnap her, Your Honour, but I am not guilty.
JUDGE 2:	How is that possible?
H.TUAH:	My ultimate aim was a noble one.
JUDGE 1:	Is it possible for an evil deed to have a noble end?
JUDGE 3:	Sounds like there is a contradiction in there somewhere.
H.TUAH:	You honour, there was in reality no evil deed. I kidnapped her so that the Sultan of Melaka could marry her. So essentially, I was doing a service to my master, the greatest *raja* of his time, the ruler of one of the most powerful port-towns in this part of the world. In fact the crime, if any, was a noble one, for it made Tun Teja into a queen. What else could any lady desire?
JUDGE 2:	How noble a deed indeed.
JUDGE 1:	Nevertheless, it was a crime against the person of Tun Teja, against her fiancé, her father the *bendahara* of Inderapura, and the *rakyat* of that state.
H.TUAH:	I disagree, Your Honour. Her marriage to my Sultan in fact brought tremendous prestige to her family and to the backward, insignificant *kampung*-state of Inderapura, no bigger than the palm of my hand, which thereby became famous. Thus, my kidnapping of the lady can ill be defined as a criminal act.

JUDGE 2:	You are mistaken, Hang Tuah. A crime remains a crime even if the end it attains is deemed noble. Even if there is benefit to some, others may be affected in a negative manner. Perhaps Melaka gained, but Inderapura suffered.
JUDGE 1:	Did you not consider the consequences of your actions?
H.TUAH:	I did, I did thoroughly, Your Honour. I planned the whole thing very carefully, consequences and all—that is why the plan worked so beautifully, like a song, one might say.
JUDGE 2:	You take pride in being a schemer?
JUDGE 3:	Sounds like our old friend Machiavelli to me. I forget, what's his first name?
H.TUAH:	Nicolo, Your Honour.
JUDGE 3:	Thanks. I wasn't sure if it was Nicolo or Picolo.
H.TUAH:	To be sure I do. There is a certain thrill in planning and executing dangerous deeds. One can live with them as pleasant memories through such events as the present ridiculous situation. Such deeds have the uncanny habit of immortalizing persons like me. Long after this trial and the completion of the present play, I will be remembered by the Malay world, *Dunia Melayu*. So, for one's courage and one's willingness to accept challenges, one is rewarded with immortality of a sort. In my case I became a legend in my own lifetime. Pirates and common thieves of both Majapahit and Melaka

feared me. Heroes on both sides of the Straits of Melaka admired me; and the women . . . . Well, there is no need to dwell on that theme. Perhaps you have already read in the *hikayat* named after me of my final disappearance into the extensive territories and boundless love of the Princess of Gunung Ledang.

JUDGE 1: Hang Tuah, will you stop beating about the bush? Please answer to the point.

H.TUAH: My humble apologies, Your Honour, I got carried away with memories of my own glory and achievements; memories, ah memories. But to answer your question briefly, yes I do take pride in being a schemer: scheming is a mark of a certain kind of uncanny super-intelligence, Your Honour.

JUDGE 2: The cheek of him!

JUDGE 3: And you say too that your loyalty and devotion to your sultan outweigh your crime of kidnapping Tun Teja.

H.TUAH: Absolutely, Your Honour, according to the Melayu way of thinking.

JUDGE 2: Rumours have it ever since your Inderapura adventure that you kidnapped Tun Teja because you yourself were in love with her. What do you have to say to that?

H.TUAH: I do not deny it, Your Honour. I believe any man in my place would have similarly succumbed to her rare heavenly beauty.

JUDGE 3:   Why then did you surrender her to your master?

H.TUAH: The Sultan had once expressed his desire to marry Tun Teja, and I considered it my duty to fulfil his every wish, no matter how trivial or whimsical, no matter what danger or inconvenience awaited me. The Sultan's happiness mattered most; that was all I lived for. Nothing, not even Tun Teja's dazzling beauty, could come between me and my vow to obtain her for my ruler.

JUDGE 1:   I put in to you, Hang Tuah, that in fact you used Tun Teja to regain the sultan's favour. She became a mere pawn in your game, the innocent victim of an intrigue which spread all the way from the Straits of Melaka to the South China Sea. Despite promises to marry her yourself, you gave her away, coldly, to your master whom she had never seen, much less wished to marry.

H.TUAH: My intentions were entirely honourable, Your Honour, I did not realize she was so beautiful.

JUDGE 2:   In other words, if you had seen Tun Teja before you made your so-called vow, you would have married her yourself. Is that correct?

H.TUAH: Certainly.

JUDGE 1:   I put it to you, Hang Tuah, that you had no plans of any sort when you left Melaka in disgrace, a refugee from death that hung over your head like an impatient scimitar; that the moment you saw Tun Teja you devised the scheme to use her to satisfy your master's lust, to obtain his pardon as well as his favours.

H.TUAH: That is not true, Your Honour. I went to Inderapura specifically to persuade Tun Teja to return to Melaka with me, so that my master could marry her.

JUDGE 2:   But remember, Hang Tuah, you left Melaka for Inderapura without your master's knowledge or blessings. The sultan could not have possibly indicated to you his desire for Tun Teja. Isn't that true?

H.TUAH: Your Honour, the Sultan had expressed his wish in passing long before I was consigned to prison, condemned to death. I took the first opportunity to serve him . . .

JUDGE 3:   As his pimp procurer, no doubt.

H.TUAH: I object to that, Your Honour. I may be a black, hypocritical villain at heart as many, nay most of us are, but I will never stoop so low as to become deserving of the title pimp.

JUDGE 3:   I withdraw my remark. Please strike it off the record. Perhaps a more suitable term to describe you would be "go-between".

H.TUAH: A loyal servant of an excellent master, Your Honour. Neither pimp, procurer nor go-between. My duties ranged far and wide. There were no specifications, no terms of reference or job descriptions in those far off days. One served one's master in the best manner, and in any capacity one could. Although I could have married Tun Teja myself, I resisted the temptation. I would have had to stay away in permanent self-exile from Melaka had I done so.

JUDGE 2: I put it to you that you wanted to be a hero. To be remembered as someone prepared to sacrifice an outstandingly beautiful lady. Your aim was a purely selfish one.

H.TUAH: That's not true. I had done enough deeds in the past to deserve all the honours, all the decorations Melaka could give me, to acquire a permanent place in the memories of my fellow-countrymen, and in history books.

JUDGE 3: But you were sentenced to death. You were meant to die with a *keris* plunged deep into your heart.

H.TUAH: Yes, but that, as they say, is another story.

JUDGE 1: How did you manage to meet Tun Teja?

H.TUAH: That's a long story, Your Honour, but to cut it short, I obtained the affection and services of a venerable old crone, Tun Teja's senior *dayang*, named Dang Rakna. She it was who brought us together.

JUDGE 3: Please give us more details.

H.TUAH: You see, Your Honour, after I came to Inderapura I spared no effort to get into the *dayang's* good books—plied her with gifts and so on. I also used the same tactics to get close to the dancers, singers and handmaidens working in the palace,

23

so that while they told me more about Tun Teja they also aroused her interest in me. To some extent, my name was already well-known outside Melaka, even on the east coast of the peninsula, owing to my heroic deeds. I tried to capitalize on that. I discovered that although Tun Teja was engaged to Megat Panji Alam, a Terengganu prince, she had neither any desire nor inclination to marry him. Indeed I believe he was old, and she detested him. So I felt secure in my plans. Dang Rakna one night arranged for me to actually see Tun Teja without her knowing it. I was completely overcome with her beauty.

JUDGE 1: But according to the *hikayat* it was she who fell in love with you.

H.TUAH: Not immediately, Your Honour. Perhaps later on she did. I used a powerful love potion and magical charms which Dang Rakna obtained for me from a well-known *bomoh*. Such charms and potions were fashionable in the *kampung*s then as they still are now.

JUDGE 3: I believe there is a revival of interest in traditional medicine, and the *bomoh* are doing well these days, even in cities like Kuala Lumpur. They can even afford to advertise in newspapers, buy fancy cars.

JUDGE 2: Go on with your story. Sounds interesting.

H.TUAH: As I was saying, I used love potions and charms to gain positive results. I could not take a chance although, thinking in retrospect, I am certain she would have eventually fallen in love with me even without them.

JUDGE 1:   And yet she married your sultan. How come?

H.TUAH: I used a countercharm to get her to fall out of love with me. It was extremely simple, you see.

JUDGE 2:   While in Inderapura, you gave her the impression that you were madly in love with her, is that it? Isn't that so?

H.TUAH: I did, Your Honour. There was nevertheless some truth in that.

JUDGE 2:   Would you not call that deception? A diabolical scheme?

H.TUAH: Perhaps, Your Honour, but I suffered too, as a consequence of what I had to do to please my master.

JUDGE 2:   How so?

H.TUAH: You see, Your Honour, I felt insanely jealous when eventually she had to marry my boss. I could not sleep; I lost weight and had to take tranquilizers. There were many in court out to create trouble for me, especially since I managed to cheat death twice. I had to watch every step, trust no one. It was agony, trying to conceal my real feelings for her, Your Honour. After all those centuries, I can still feel the pangs of love.

JUDGE 2:   There were persistent rumours that you had an affair with her while in Inderapura. What do you say to that?

H.TUAH:	There's absolutely no truth in them. It would have been too dangerous and not in keeping with court *adat*. I worshipped her as a devotee worships his favourite idol, Your Honour, but alas only from a distance.
JUDGE 2:	You mentioned dangers. What sort of dangers?
H.TUAH:	I would have lost my head, *kaput* (*makes a sign*). So I had to suffer in silence. I wrote a great many *pantun*. My manuscript has not as yet been discovered. It lies buried somewhere, with the constant turmoil Melaka has seen. But who knows, one day some archaeological expedition from Museum Negara or one of the universities may recover those relics from my past, and the *pantun* may yet get published.
JUDGE 2:	So you sacrificed a true love in the way of loyalty?
H.TUAH:	I certainly did, Your Honour.
JUDGE 3:	But why? I really don't understand. Sounds crazy.
H.TUAH:	Those were strange times, Your Honour. Any refusal to conform would have resulted in charges of treason, *derhaka*. Believe me, there is no greater crime in the Melayu mind. There was very little choice. One had to leave one's haven, sail endlessly in Sinbad the Sailor-fashion looking for alternative places to settle, or suffer the common penalty: death. Nor was there even the option of a noble death through *hara-kiri*. After all, we were not Japanese.

JUDGE 1: Coming back to the kidnapping, did you not feel you committed offence against anyone?

H.TUAH: I did; I did, Your Honour. It was certainly unfair for me to treat the *bendahara* of Inderapura in that manner, running away with his daughter in the still darkness of night. Perhaps, indirectly, I committed some offence against Megat Panji Alam, the old Terengganu clown who was hoping to marry Tun Teja. I am sure they both felt terribly humiliated by her escape. I was especially remorseful for what I did to Tun Teja's father. Later on, I wrote him a note of apology; I also sent a Hari Raya card and a bouquet of flowers. For Megat Panji Alam I had no sympathies. I don't think he deserved Tun Teja. It's not surprising that she did not want him. You see, he was not even immortal in the true sense of the word. According to most accounts, he was a jerk.

JUDGE 3: It appears in your bio data that you studied black magic from some mountain-top guru. Did you use such magic on Tun Teja?

H.TUAH: Your Honour, I only studied a special variety of magic for self-defence, for use in war. My teacher was a venerable Javanese *kyai*. Through it, I was on several occasions able to save the lives of the Sultan and my close companions. The only magic I used on Tun Teja was what I obtained from my adoptive mother in Pahang, Dang Rakna. I was never a fully qualified *bomoh*. I must admit, though, that on occasions my innate personal charm worked wonders.

JUDGE 2:   Some recent newspaper articles have expressed the opinion that a trial such as this has been overdue by centuries. Hence these proceedings are likely to cause a sensation.

JUDGE 1:   Every community needs every now and then to re-examine its character, reassess its identity. Such an exercise can help in removing cobwebs, letting in a breath of fresh air.

H.TUAH: I could not agree more, Your Honour. Only I wonder why they have started on the wrong foot in my case—by assuming that I am guilty of so many absurd crimes.

JUDGE 2:   A mere starting point. How otherwise can a proper post-mortem be conducted? But remember, you are innocent until proven guilty.

JUDGE 1:   The conscience of society, so to speak, has been receiving an airing.

H.TUAH: Believe me, I am not enjoying these lengthy sessions of intense probing. It's all so ridiculous.

JUDGE 3:   Remember, Hang Tuah, you can be charged with contempt of court if you go on in that vein, hero or no hero.

H.TUAH: But I *am* a hero; I have long been a hero, and I will always remain one. Can anyone doubt that?

SCENE 5

The court-house, as before. Tun Teja is in the witness stand. Young, elegant, and extremely beautiful, she is dressed in modern clothes which show good taste and high fashion. It is obvious that she is avoiding looking at Hang Tuah.

JUDGE 1:   Your name please.

TUN TEJA: Tun Teja.

JUDGE 3:   Is Teja a short form for Khatijah, as in Khatijah binti Awang? You know the famous *mak yong* actress.

TUN TEJA: No, I don't, Your Honour. Tun Teja is my full name.

JUDGE 1:   Please give us your age and occupation.

Tun Teja remains silent, shy.

JUDGE 2:   O, let's forget about these details. You see the lady is blushing. I presume everyone here has done some homework—read the *Hikayat Hang Tuah* and so on. All the details are in that work.

TUN TEJA: Thank you, Your Honour, you are very kind indeed.

JUDGE 2:	My pleasure, Miss. Now tell us, Tun Teja, do you recognize this man here?

TUN TEJA:	(*Looking briefly at Hang Tuah*). Yes, Your Honour.

JUDGE 1:	How intimately do you know him?

Tun Teja does not answer.

JUDGE 3:	Answer the question, Tun Teja.

TUN TEJA:	I do not think it proper to speak of such things in public, Your Honour.

JUDGE 2:	Would you like this section of the hearing to be heard in camera, then, Miss?

TUN TEJA:	It's alright, Your Honour. There's nothing sordid about is, it's just that the wording of the question . . .

JUDGE 3:	Alright then, let us phrase the question in a different manner, to make it more comfortable. Do you know the defendant here very intimately, fairly intimately, casually, or not at all? Think of this as an objective test and tick, I mean pick, one of the answers. Which one will it be?

Tun Teja remains silent.

JUDGE 1:	What is it, Tun Teja? Are you afraid there will be a scandal, the details will be printed in tomorrow's newspapers, announced over the TV?

TUN TEJA:	That's not it, Your Honour.

JUDGE 2:   What then? Speak up and tell us.

TUN TEJA: You see, the whole thing was so beautiful, so romantic, almost like a fairy tale . . .

JUDGE 3:   Yes, go on.

TUN TEJA: By bringing it to this court room every detail meant to be confidential . . .

JUDGE 3:   I see . . . you mean it will be like washing dirty linen in public.

TUN TEJA: Not exactly, Your Honour, there's no dirty linen involved. Private matters will be brought into the public domain, beauty will be lost, like perfume escapes from a bottle of Chanel 5 when left uncovered. After some time, with the fragrance gone, the elegant perfume becomes a foul unworthy liquid fit only for the drain or wash basin.

JUDGE 2:   Your point is well-taken, but I am afraid we cannot avoid some of this exposure, the accusations levelled against the defendant are serious. I hope you will co-operate with this bench so that truth may be prised out. Hang Tuah's reputation, even his life depends on this trial. Knowing his legendary stature, the historic nature of this futuristic trial, and the varying impressions left upon different groups of observers and readers of the *hikayat*, this house would like to establish the truth as soon as possible. The inquisitors would like to have your co-operation in the matter. We assure you that the intention of this assembly is neither to open old wounds, not to embarrass anyone. I hope therefore that you will understand the situation, help the jury in arriving at a judgment.

TUN TEJA: Your Honour, I was intimidated by the word "intimately".

JUDGE 1: Is that all? (*Tun Teja nods*). Well, then, we'll phrase it differently, leave out the intimidating word. You said earlier you recognized this man. Did you know him very well?

TUN TEJA: (*Nodding*) Not really, Your Honour.

JUDGE 1: Well, now that's been taken care of, perhaps we can proceed with this historical and futuristic trial.

JUDGE 2: Good, that's a start.

JUDGE 3: Tun Teja, Hang Tuah was in Melaka and you in Inderapura. Did you know him before he went to Inderapura?

TUN TEJA: No, Your Honour. I had heard about Melaka and things happening there. His name did pop up once or twice. Apparently, he was quite well known.

JUDGE 2: So I take it there was no direct contact between the two of you. There wasn't any kind of correspondence. Is that true?

TUN TEJA: True, Your Honour. I did not even know him then, and there was no reason for me to write to him. I saw him for the first time when he came to Inderapura.

JUDGE 1:   Go on. Tell us more.

TUN TEJA: His fame had already travelled well ahead of him, and when he came to Inderapura the men admired him because he was such an all-rounder . . .

JUDGE 3:   All-rounder?

TUN TEJA: Yes, Your Honour. He was a warrior, and could play *sepak raga* very well. He could also perform *silat*, recite *pantun*, sing and tell stories. The news about his arrival, and his many accomplishments travelled fast. The men, especially the young ones, admired him for his many skills.

JUDGE 2:   And what about the women? How did they react to his arrival in Inderapura?

TUN TEJA: Your Honour, the women were certainly excited. I believe some of the women found him highly attractive.

JUDGE 1:   What about you, Tun Teja? Did you too find him attractive?

TUN TEJA: Not particularly, Your Honour. At least not in the beginning. I saw him play *sepak raga* from my window once, and knew he was the newcomer from Melaka, but I did not feel anything for him. He was skilful, but in his looks, he was in no way outstanding; certainly not a Dilip Kumar or a Shahrukh Khan.

JUDGE 3: How would you rate him, for his handsomeness on a scale of ten?

TUN TEJA: (*After some hesitation*) Somewhere in the middle, perhaps five, at most six.

JUDGE 2: So in your opinion, he was merely average in his looks?

TUN TEJA: That is correct, Your Honour.

JUDGE 1: Did you know anything else about him apart from the little information you have given this court?

TUN TEJA: Yes, Your Honour. My senior *dayang*, Dang Rakna, who had adopted Hang Tuah as her "son" provided me with some further information. I understood from her remarks that she liked him very much; that he was kind to her, plying her with gifts and so on. On the whole, her comments built up the defendant's stature, so that he seemed kind-hearted, generous, and heroic. She elaborated on his adventures and exploits, some of which had been familiar to me from other sources. I was not sure, of course, if all the stories she related to me were true. I got the impression, on the whole, that she admired him unreservedly, was prepared to do anything for him.

JUDGE 2: Did it occur to you then, that possibly the man from Melaka was using her to obtain your favour? That all the flattery was intended to arouse your interest in Hang Tuah?

JUDGE 3: To press his suit, so to speak.

TUN TEJA: No, Your Honour. It did not occur to me that such was her intention.

JUDGE 2: Did you not so much as suspect it?

TUN TEJA: No, Your Honour. I had known Dang Rakna for many, many years, had complete faith in her. She was like a mother to me.

JUDGE 3: When did you find out that in fact she had been working for him and trying to entrap you?

TUN TEJA: Much, much later. After I had married the sultan of Melaka.

JUDGE 1: That's a big jump. Let's take it a little at a time, so that the members of this august assembly can follow the events closely. Now, tell the bench how you met Hang Tuah, gained confidence in him to the extent of becoming willing to run away with him. It's true, isn't it that you ran away, rather eloped, with him to Melaka?

TUN TEJA: It's like this, Your Honour. Dang Rakna and my other attendants kept telling me good things about Hang Tuah, singing his praises. Then one evening as I was alone in my room, with my maidens, practicing a dance . . .

JUDGE 3: Ah, so you have interest in the performing arts?

TUN TEJA: Yes, Your Honour. I do a little dancing and occasionally play the gamelan, just to pass time. I also sometimes watch *bangsawan*, even though it's not a great art form at all. I prefer *mak yong* or *wayang kulit*.

JUDGE 2:   Go on.

TUN TEJA: As I said, I was with my handmaidens, and . . .

The scene changes to the Inderapura in the 15ᵗʰ century. It is evening and Tun Teja is in her house with Dang Rakna and several other two principal dayang, Susi and Santi. There is some traditional music being played in the background. Tun Teja is lying on a couch, reading a copy of Cosmopolitan magazine, while two dayangs are fanning her. Tun Teja puts down her magazine and sits up on her couch, sighing.

TUN TEJA: *Dayang*, please ask them to stop playing the music.

D.RAKNA: Tun Teja, my child, why is it that for several days now we have seen you so melancholic and lost as if your mind is somewhere far off?

Dang Rakna offers Tun Teja a quid of betel-leaves. Tun Teja takes it and puts it in her mouth.

TUN TEJA: I have no idea, *dayang*. It seems as if some dark and mysterious vapour coming with the southwest wind causes these bouts of depression.

SUSI: Could it be a problem, my Lady? Some worry you can share with your companions. Sharing one's burdens has the effect of making them bearable, for each sharer takes a portion, and the whole thereby becomes lighter.

D.RAKNA: Problems? Why talk of problems my friend? Problems come and problems go, but persons have to remain. Problems are meant to be solved, and there are few if any without solutions. One just has to try hard, that's all.

TUN TEJA: If there's no other solution, then one just waits for death, the final answer to all problems.

D.RAKNA: Do not talk of death, my child. You have a long and beautiful life before you. You are still very young, a fresh bud just beginning to unfold, bursting to be plucked. Death is real only to old crones like me.

TUN TEJA: Some people die a living death, *dayang*.

D.RAKNA: Once you were as lively as the young spring that bounces off the rocks as it tumbles down into the river, creating in its process beautiful rainbows, melodious streams, their music carried far and wide on vaporous winds. What could have happened to change all that, I wonder?

SANTI: Perhaps my Lady is nervous.

D.RAKNA: Nervous about what?

SUSI: Well you know, about the proposal from Megat Panji Alam. There is a great deal of excitement in the air. In the *dayangs'* quarters, all the talk is about the impending wedding.

TUN TEJA: What wedding? *Dayang, dayang*, please don't go on and on. Have I not told you before to stop mentioning that name in my presence?

SANTI: Perhaps my Lady would like to hear the latest gossip in the *dayangs'* quarters, then?

TUN TEJA: Is there anything that can happen in a dull place like this?

D.RAKNA: Oh, but my Lady, this time it is quite different. Much is happening, but perhaps it doesn't concern my Lady. Here, have some chocolate, my Lady.

TUN TEJA: Chocolate! (*Taking it*) What a strange thing! What do I do with it?

D.RAKNA: Eat it, of course. What else?

TUN TEJA: (*Eating*) What a strange thing; but is quite good. Where did this come from, *dayang*?

D.RAKNA: Here, have another piece, my Lady. It's imported; came by special delivery from far off Melaka.

TUN TEJA: From Melaka?

SUSI: Oh I see. You get chocolate and other goodies and keep them all to yourself, do you?

D.RAKNA: I've just unpacked the boxes, my dear. So, don't accuse me of being selfish. I'll give you some later on. But this is of a super-special variety. It's special, and it's meant only for my Lady.

TUN TEJA: Who brought you this chocolate, *dayang*?

SANTI: Perhaps the lady is not aware, there is a great deal of talk about a newcomer from Melaka.

D.RAKNA: Yes, my Lady. It's from the newcomer, Hang Tuah. He sends it to you with his compliments and the season's greetings.

TUN TEJA: Thank you, *dayang*. Give my thanks to the visitor. Tell him we hope he has a pleasant stay here in Inderapura.

SUSI: My Lady, the town is abuzz with chatter, there's excitement amongst the young maidens about this new arrival. It seems he is generous, a great giver of gifts, and a talented *sepak raga* player.

SANTI: His bravery and heroism have become legendary in the seas surrounding these Malay kingdoms. It seems as if he's been fighting battles against the enemies of Melaka ever since childhood, like one born with a magical *keris* in his hand, so deftly he handles that weapon . . .

D.RAKNA: His deeds, my Lady, have been written in *hikayat* that will be read by generations to come. It seems they are also performed in famous *bangsawan* and *sandiwara* theatres in Penang and Singapore . . .

SUSI: And his *ilmu* . . . it seems as if anyone looking at him develops an instant liking for him. He studied with a famous *kyai*, a hermit in Majapahit.

TUN TEJA: *Dayang*, you certainly seem to have discovered a great deal about him, and so soon too.

SUSI: I couldn't help it, my Lady. *Everyone* without exception is talking about him.

D.RAKNA: I've never ever in my many, many years met a kinder, more generous person, my Lady. Here, have another piece of chocolate.

TUN TEJA: Thank you, *dayang*. (*Taking one*) It's really super. But tell me, why do you go on and on with descriptions of his person and character, *dayang*?

SANTI: It's his personality, my Lady. He's very unusual, like a star suddenly coming into view in the dark Inderapura sky.

D.RAKNA: We thought perhaps our Lady would like to hear about him, this brave and handsome warrior from the West. It seems, my Lady that your father the *bendahara*, regards him very highly, and has even invited him to visit some time.

TUN TEJA: Really?

SUSI: And Dang Rakna is so impressed with him that she's adopted him as her son. There seems to have developed instant rapport between the two, isn't that so?

D.RAKNA: He makes it a point to visit me every evening, lady, after *maghrib*; spends several hours at my humble hut.

TUN TEJA: I have heard. Obviously, you like him a lot.

SUSI: Of course, with him calling her 'mother' and providing her extraordinary gifts.

D.RAKNA: It seems his master, the sultan of Melaka, is very noble indeed. He himself is extremely refined, *halus* in his manners, like Arjuna or Seri Rama.

SANTI: I have never seen him, myself, but I am told he's not bad looking. Perhaps Dang Rakna here can describe him or bring along a photograph of his, so that my Lady can take a look.

TUN TEJA: But I *have* seen him.

D.RAKNA: Seen him? When? Where?

TUN TEJA: Several days ago, when he was playing *sepak raga* and demonstrating *silat* movements in the *medan* outside my window.

D.RAKNA: Lady, you've seen him and yet you have remained silent all this while. And here we go on and on talking about him. Is he fair or dark, handsome or ugly, my Lady? What do you think?

TUN TEJA: He's not much to look at, *dayang*; just about average.

SUSI: You must be teasing, lady. The maidens of this town are all athrill with his arrival, and you say he's average.

TUN TEJA: Well, perhaps a little above average, but certainly nothing to shout about.

D.RAKNA: Is that so?

SANTI: What do *you* think, Dang Rakna?

D.RAKNA: I think he's really handsome. Perhaps, when my Lady sees him at close quarters, she will change her impressions about him. After all, she's only seen him at a distance from the window.

SUSI: Is it the newcomer, then, that has caused my Lady to be thus melancholy?

D.RAKNA: Now that you say so, I can believe it. We must arrange a meeting, and who knows the melancholia will disappear . . . just as dark clouds disappear when the sun comes out shining.

TUN TEJA: *Dayang, dayang,* must you go on and on about him. Let's do something else?

SANTI: The princess is blushing, see.

TUN TEJA: Stop teasing, you . . . you . . . (*about to pinch her, as dayang runs off*).

D.RAKNA: Lady, shall I ask the singers to entertain you.

TUN TEJA: No, you sing a song, some old fashioned melody maybe something from *mak yong* . . .

D.RAKNA: Who wants to hear this old crone sing? Anyway I don't know *mak yong* songs. You see, I am not from Patani or Kelantan. No, princess, you dance.

TUN TEJA: I'm not in the mood.

SUSI: The dance will restore your mood, princess, drive away the sadness, and if that doesn't work,

42

then we'll just have to ask *Dayang* Rakna here to introduce you to her adopted son. Perhaps, she can bring him here on some pretext or other. To tell you of the mighty kingdom of Melaka and its sultan.

TUN TEJA: Wait till I catch you, *dayang*.

D.RAKNA: Shall I ask the musicians to play, lady, so that you can dance?

SUSI: Of course. The princess will dance.

Dang Rakna signals the musicians while Tun Teja threatens dayang. Tun Teja dances solo, a slow dance. Hang Tuah, who has been watching and overhearing the conversation from behind a curtain, enters. When the dance is over, he claps and applauds loudly. Tun Teja, embarrassed, rushes to take her scarf and quickly covers her head.

H.TUAH: Bravo, bravo, a beautiful number, an enchanting dancer. It seems that a *bidadari* descended from the *kayangan* to perform specially for me.

D.RAKNA: Laksmana, you are most welcome. Please sit down.

SUSI: Yes, do sit down. The lady will be here as soon as she has caught her breath and finished blushing. We are leaving, lady.

TUN TEJA: No, *dayang*, don't leave me alone. Don't desert me.

H.TUAH: Lady, a small token of appreciation for your sensational dance. (*Offers her a bouquet of flowers, but Tun Teja hesitates to come near him or to accept it.)* Come on, lady. I am just another human being, and not a monster descended from some wild mountain. I will neither offend nor harm you, I can assure you. My name is Laksamana Hang Tuah, and I come from far off Melaka of international fame. O, I beg your pardon, thus intruding upon you unannounced. I happened to be passing your window, heard the heavenly strains; I thought I would pause awhile, refresh myself with the music, and then move on. *(Tun Teja remains silent)*. My Lady, if my presence offends you, I shall take my leave now. But please accept these flowers.

TUN TEJA: No, no. Stay awhile. *(Takes the flowers, and smells them.)* Thank you.

She comes nearer and sits down some distance away from him. He too sits. A dayang enters with drinks for Hang Tuah and placing them on a small table, leaves, but not before teasing Tun Teja, Tun Teja threatens her.

Lights dim out and come on again as at the beginning of the scene. Tun Teja is still at the witness stand.

TUN TEJA: I discovered that Hang Tuah had been watching me all along. I felt so embarrassed. Since he had come to my house, I could not chase him away or leave. That would have been highly discourteous, against our *adat*. I guessed his presence there came about as a result of a plan hatched by Dang Rakna. It seemed like his idea too, Your Honour, to surprise me at my place.

JUDGE 2:   So you were not angry or upset about the intrusion?

TUN TEJA: It naturally came to me as a shock to discover Hang Tuah in my house. I was nervous, in case my father came to know of his visit. But there was little I could do. So I let him stay awhile, offered him food and drink. After that, he thanked me heartily and went off.

JUDGE 3:   Did you fall head over heels in love with him at that encounter?

TUN TEJA: No, Your Honour, of course not. Such things only happen in fairy tales or Hindustani movies. Several days later, Dang Rakna invited me to have dinner with him, saying that he wanted very much to meet me. I resisted, but again, pitying the stranger who had come from so far way beyond the waters, I went to Dang Rakna's house. We met several times in this manner; thus, gradually I began to know him a little better.

JUDGE 1:   Then how come you decided to elope with him? That hardly seems logical if you had only known him a little.

TUN TEJA: Your Honour, frankly, I did not know what was happening to me. As the days passed, Hang Tuah's presence began to grow upon me, and I found myself increasingly attracted to him. Before long, I was in love with him, and so when he suggested that we elope, I saw it as an opportunity to escape from marriage with Megat Panji Alam. Thus, one dark night Hang Tuah, Dang Rakna, and I escaped in a boat to Malacca.

JUDGE 2:   Did you know at that time, that during the days when Hang Tuah was supposedly "courting" you, he was in fact using magical charms to cause you to fall in love with him.

TUN TEJA: (*Shocked*) Is that so? I was not aware of that, Your Honour. This is the first time I have heard such a thing.

JUDGE 3:   Could the chocolate you ate have something to do with it?

TUN TEJA: Coming to think of it, Your Honour, perhaps it did. That explains a great deal of what was happening to me—my sudden change of heart and so on. It could, of course, also have been some *mantera*, or some sort of dark, and mysterious knowledge he had acquired.

JUDGE 3:   To return to your story. Tell us what happened in Melaka.

TUN TEJA: Once *Dayang* Rakna and I reached Melaka with him, I noticed that the Laksamana was deliberately avoiding me. Soon, the news reached me that I was to marry the sultan. I was extremely distressed, Your Honour.

JUDGE 2:   Yet you married the sultan.

TUN TEJA: I had no choice, Your Honour. What else could I have done? I felt cheated, deserted, totally humiliated by the treatment the Laksamana gave me. It was nothing short of deception particularly, as you point out, Your Honour, he used magical charms to make me fall in love with him. I believe he then used counter-charms to neutralize their effect. The whole thing was so inhuman. Gradually, however, as I came to know the sultan and my devotion for Hang Tuah seemed to mysteriously vanish, I felt it wasn't such a bad idea after all to marry the ruler of Melaka. The only alternative was for me to go home to Inderapura in disgrace to face the wrath of my father and Megat Panji Alam himself.

JUDGE 1:   Just to backtrack a little, would you have been willing to leave Inderapura with Hang Tuah, if, in the first instance, he had revealed to you that he came courting you on behalf of his master?

TUN TEJA: Certainly not, Your Honour. I had not consented to my proposed marriage to Megat Panji Alam. If I wanted to marry a member of royalty, there were suitors galore in Inderapura, Kelantan, Patani, and Terengganu, Your Honour. There was no necessity for me to go all the way to Melaka to find a royal husband.

JUDGE 2:   Are you saying, therefore, that your real intention in coming to Melaka was to marry Hang Tuah, and not the sultan or anyone else?

TUN TEJA: Yes, Your Honour. It was in some way impetuous, given the circumstances, but that is correct.

JUDGE 1:   But in the process you got deceived by Hang Tuah, when he offered you as a mere gift to his master. Isn't that true?

TUN TEJA: Yes, Your Honour.

JUDGE 2:   What were your feelings then?

TUN TEJA: I felt betrayed, helpless, completely lost. I was on the verge of insanity owing to the disgrace I experienced, Your Honour.

JUDGE 1:   Because you were used cruelly by Hang Tuah as a mere tool for his own ends, is that it?

TUN TEJA: I wasn't aware of Hang Tuah's motives at first. Later on, I learnt at the harem in Melaka that in fact he had used me to regain the sultan's favour. That his trip to Inderapura had been undertaken precisely to bring me back to Melaka by hook or by crook so that by using me, he could get his death sentence commuted. I felt used, like some soulless object, for his evil design.

JUDGE 2:   So in effect your elopement with Hang Tuah, although apparently done willingly, was not so, since you were charmed?

TUN TEJA: Yes, Your Honour. I think you have clearly seen my situation.

JUDGE 1:   Would "kidnapping" be an accurate description of what happened to you?

TUN TEJA: Yes, Your Honour, exactly so.

JUDGE 2:   Did Hang Tuah ever ask you to marry him, either before or after the elopement?

TUN TEJA: Never, Your Honour, not once.

JUDGE 3:	Did he ever, even indirectly, give any indication that he was going to marry you?
TUN TEJA:	No, Your Honour, not the vaguest hint. I was so blindly in love with him. I assumed his request to me to elope with him was tantamount to a proposal of marriage.
JUDGE 3:	Did you know that he already had a couple of wives in Melaka?
TUN TEJA:	I did not, Your Honour. This is the first time I am hearing such thing. I never even thought of that possibility.
JUDGE 2:	In other words, you were so completely charmed by his character, your confidence in him was so total that you did not even imagine he was deceiving you. Would that be correct?
TUN TEJA:	Yes, Your Honour, exactly.
JUDGE 1:	Suppose I put it to you that you married the sultan because you saw the golden opportunity to become sultana in the most powerful town of the time; that you did it because of your ambition, and that you dumped Hang Tuah?
TUN TEJA:	That's not true, Your Honour. I did not love the sultan of Melaka despite his fame, his money, and his power. I would not have been the sultana as he had several wives and concubines. I was totally helpless. I had been abandoned in a foreign land after being led by Hang Tuah along the garden path, so to speak, with false protestations of love.

JUDGE 2:   Just one final question. Supposing you had your life to live all over again, and knowing the background and character of Hang Tuah, would you be willing to consider marrying him?

TUN TEJA: Never, Your Honour. I have already told the court I was not at all impressed with him. The pain of deception, the agony of rejection; they were totally unbearable. After all these centuries, I still feel it in my heart. No, Your Honour, thanks but no thanks.

Lights fade out. Exit everyone.

SCENE 6

Melaka, the sultan's palace. The announcer enters, only his face is lit by a spotlight. His words are also clearly displayed on a signboard.

ANNOUNCER: Fifteenth century Melaka, a town at its glorious best. As a result of Hang Tuah's being sentenced to death, Hang Jebat has taken over the palace and the sultan has left with his entourage to stay at the Datuk Bedahara's house. Hang Tuah, who in fact is not dead, returns, and upon the sultan's orders goes to challenge Hang Jebat, with the intention of killing him. Despite Hang Jebat's pleas, based upon the issues of personal devotion, friendship, and the blind loyalty of Hang Tuah towards the sultan, Hang Tuah is unmoved. The famous duel between the two heroes takes place. Hang Jebat is killed by Hang Tuah. (*Exit*)

When lights come on, Hang Jebat is seen in the sultan's palace with Dang Wangi and other court ladies. There is music, much laughter as well as other activities indicating an atmosphere of gaiety and celebration.

H.JEBAT: Now ladies, let us not indulge ourselves too much, though a surfeit of love did no one any harm.

The ladies feed him with grapes and other fruits, ply him with drinks.

H.JEBAT: (*Taking a sip*) And the sultan, I mean the tyrant, did he drink this too? I always wondered what kind of heavenly nectar trickled down his supposedly blue-veined throat. (*Laughter*) Come, you can tell me. It is very unlikely he will overhear. I see he has already run off to the *bendahara*'s house. The coward!

D.WANGI: Don't let him hear that. He'll come for your blood.

H.JEBAT: Unlikely. If he had the courage he would have stayed on here in the first place to defend his palace and all you pretty ladies. Or having left, he would have come back by now. I have seen a great deal of him, and one thing he does not have, in my opinion, is courage.

LADY 1: Remember his *keris*, Datuk.

H.JEBAT: *Keris*? Huh. Don't be stupid, my dear. What can a *keris* do without the courage to back it up, the physical strength, and the grace in the wrist? Nothing. No wonder he is still sitting there in exile in the *bendahara*'s *kampung*, away from his palace, his concubines, and mistresses, all the tinsel trappings of majesty, perhaps hoping for some kind of a royal miracle. And now that Hang Tuah is dead, and I no longer support him, what can he do? There will be no more miracles in Melaka, except for me.

D.WANGI: Do you plan to become the sultan?

H.JEBAT: I haven't had time to think about it, my dear; have been too busy. You ladies should know that. But

I wonder if it is really worth it. How many kings or sultans, how many maharajas or emperors have been remembered fondly in history? Not more than a clutch of them, I'm certain. We can count them on the fingers of a single hand. Perhaps hundreds have been assassinated, dispatched by the hands of those closest to them. Come on, let's forget politics for a while. Let me enjoy myself. I have spent a great deal of time and energy for others. It is about time I thought of myself. More drink! More drink, and music! Yes, let's have music and dancing girls.

He claps several times. Dancing girls enter from all directions. A seductive Arabian Nights fantasy dance is performed, while Jebat behaves quite indecorously. He should not, however, be portrayed as someone without restraint. At the end of the dance, he applauds. As the music and laughter subside, the voice of Hang Tuah is heard. The dancing girls move away, nervously, and everyone else present is suddenly quiet, tense.

H.JEBAT: Fantastic: out of this world.

H.TUAH: Jebat, you traitor . . .

H.JEBAT: (*Rising suddenly, his hand going to his keris*). Who dares call me traitor? Traitor to whom? To this effeminate sultan of Melaka? No, I am no traitor. Did anyone else hear someone call my name? (*He looks around and all stand dumbfounded.*)

D.WANGI: It . . . it sounded like the voice of the Laksmana, Datuk.

LADY 2:   Perhaps his spirit has come back from the dead . . . to haunt Melaka, Datuk.

53

H.JEBAT:	That's impossible. You have been reading too many Singapore ghost stories. And . . . even if it were the ghost of Tuah why should it call me traitor? Pooh, a traitor? Who's the traitor, me? And who has done so much to defy the sultan, to hurt him, for the sake of a friend? Give me another example from history. A traitor? No, must be some raving lunatic just escaped from Tanjung Rambutan. Let's not think about it. Music, let's have more music. (*Music begins again; loud banging on the door is heard*)
H.TUAH:	Jebat, you traitor . . . open up and let me in.

The music stops and everyone freezes in terror. Hang Jebat alone moves slowly and towards the window.

H.JEBAT:	(*Calmly as if to himself*) It looks like him, it sounds like him, but it cannot be. It must be my imagination. My own inner fears brimming to the top, as the psychiatrists will say. My unconscious Freudian fears. Yet, what has all this to do with Freud? And fears? What fears? What fears can the mighty Jebat have? None. No, I have no fears. Perhaps I have had too much to drink, but no liquor, even though there is plenty around.
D.WANGI:	Ah, but remember, my dear, coconut juice when fermented becomes toddy, I mean Niracola; and then strange happenings can take place . . .
H.JEBAT:	My eyes. My ears, all my senses must be deceiving me. That thing out there cannot be real. No, it cannot be real.

LADY 1:   But *we* are not drunk, Datuk. We too heard it distinctly, the voice of the Laksmana, somewhat weakened, but still his. There can be no mistaking.

H.TUAH: Jebat, are you such a coward, besides being a traitor? Open up if you are a man.

H.JEBAT: It *is* my dear friend alright. Who else would dare call Jebat a coward? It is the privilege of friends to thus insult each other in jest, and then to embrace in the closest of friendships. There is nothing more beautiful in the world. Ah Tuah, so you are not dead after all. You are no unsubstantial apparition, no ghost of Hamlet's father come to mock me, to demand revenge. I *have* started my revenge on your behalf, my friend, my dead . . . and yet alive friend, revenge designed to take me to the deepest pit of hell, the highest of the seven heavens. I will, for you, fathom every ocean, climb every mountain, traverse every desert . . . if only your ghost . . . ghost? Did I say ghost? Yes, if only your ghost will find peace in the next world.

H.TUAH: Jebat, open up.

D.WANGI: He sounds impatient, Datuk and I . . . I'm getting nervous just wondering why he's so angry.

LADY 2:   He calls, Datuk, he calls.

H.JEBAT: Yes, yes, he calls; he calls like the deepest voice of our conscience, our tortured souls. He calls, he comes, but why does he come in this fashion, a manner so rugged and fearful, like revenge itself?

H.TUAH: Jebat, Jebat.

H.JEBAT: I come, my brother, I come. Even if you should call me into the longest night of burning hell, I will gladly come. I come to receive you with open arms, whether you are real, Tuah . . . or merely his shadow. Open the portals, prepare a welcome worthy of a long lost brother, a worthy friend, the mightiest hero Melaka ever saw or will see. Sound the bugle and welcome, welcome him like a king! O, you fair maidens of Melaka, go, go and bring him in with flowers. Flowers for his hair, flowers for his feet. Let not the ground hurt them. A radiant shower of flowers for my beloved friend, my brother!

Music, and some people go to bring Hang Tuah in. The maidens of the palace shower flowers on him, and before him. He is brought in a hero and received accordingly by Jebat, who embraces him as soon as he enters. Hang Tuah looks pale and now has grown a slight beard.

H.JEBAT: Ah, Tuah, you *are* real. You are not dead, not dead, my brother.

H.TUAH: No, not dead, not dead.

Hang Jebat brings him in by the hand and offers him the seat of honour. Hang Tuah hesitates to sit for a while. Hang Jebat too remains standing, waiting. Hang Tuah then sits down, and Jebat does so after him. Fruit-trays and drinks are offered to him; at first Tuah hesitates, then takes a little.

H.JEBAT: I still cannot believe this. That you are *real*, that you are not a mere ghost or spirit. Eat, my friend, eat and drink. You look weakened. Enjoy the sultan's hospitality . . . (*nervous laughter*) I was merely joking.

H.TUAH: Even though I come in anger, I cannot refuse such fine hospitality given in the ancient fashion of Melaka, the time-honoured tradition of this land of Parameswara.

H.JEBAT: Anger? Did I hear you say anger? You used strange words, my brother? Words that should not pass between two as close as we have always been. What cause is there for anger, Tuah?

H.TUAH: Cause enough and more.

H.JEBAT: Do not confuse me, Tuah. I am already overwhelmed with your return. But first things first. Tell me . . . those rumours about your death . . .

H.TUAH: Mere rumours, as you can see for yourself. Not an iota of truth in them.

H.JEBAT: Yes, it is obvious you did no die. Although, for some time, when I heard you call standing outside these palace walls, I did not believe you were real. You were to me a phantom, insubstantial shape returned from the other side of midnight to seek revenge against the tyrant, sultan Mansur Shah . . .

H.TUAH: You mean His Majesty Sultan Mansur Shah, I suppose?

H.JEBAT:	(*Nervous laughter*) Of course, I do. I did not realize you had such reverence for an enemy, a tyrant who so unjustly sent you off to the gallows for whatever reason—mere jealousy, I believe, over some woman or other.
H.TUAH:	That's enough. I shall not hear my ruler insulted in this manner.
H.JEBAT:	I understand you, Tuah. I know you were always a little whimsical from the early days, but you had style, you had courage, and above all, you had principles. I should hope you still have them.
H.TUAH:	Yes, yes, I have always upheld my principles, and I still do. Nothing has changed.
H.JEBAT:	I am glad to hear that. Now tell me, what *really* happened? How come you are still alive? And whence have you emerged so suddenly after so long?
H.TUAH:	All that is well-known in history. Just ask anyone in this theatre; even the littlest child. They can tell you. They are quite familiar with all that transpired.
H.JEBAT:	Now, I am truly confused. I don't understand a word of what you are saying—the theatre, the audience. I did feel you had lost your mind, the way you were shouting for me out there. Alas, my friend, too true what I feared. Perhaps you need psychiatric help, talk to someone; after all, you have been through a great deal. Yet, don't worry, I will take care of you, and Dang Wangi here too. You must be tired. A shower, a

long rest, and some hot soup *kambing* will soon restore you.

D.WANGI: The palace maidens will comfort you, provide for your every need, Laksmana.

LADY 1:   Yes, Laksmana Tuah.

Hang Jebat claps, and signaling to some servants, sends them off to carry out his orders. He puts his arm around Hang Tuah's shoulders as if to comfort him.

H.TUAH: (*Jumping up*) Don't play games with me, Jebat. I will not be deceived. I am not a ghost as you would like to believe. Nor am I insane as you would like to presume. I know exactly what I am doing.

H.JEBAT: And what, if I may ask, is that?

H.TUAH: I came here to kill you, Jebat, to take revenge on behalf of my master, His Majesty Sultan Mansur Shah.

D.WANGI: No, that cannot be.

H.JEBAT: I can't believe this. You must be joking.

H.TUAH: To restore him to his rightful place as the royal, respected, undisputed, God-ordained Sultan of Melaka and all its territories. This is no fantasy, no theatre, Jebat. I am as real as anyone could possibly be; no mere actor depicting myself.

H.JEBAT: Amazing! And what, if I may be told, has been my crime, to be thus deserving of an angry visit

59

from the bravest and noblest of Melaka's heroes, the flower of living mankind? This palace and all it contains, you can have it back any time, for your master or for yourself—a mere façade. It's not worth fighting for; and I have never disputed that Mansur Shah rightly or wrongly is still, for better or for worse, the sultan of Malacca.

H.TUAH: You have committed unpardonable crimes against his Majesty and the royal family, Jebat; against the sacred soil of Melaka, its people, and its equally sacred traditions. For those crimes, you must be punished.

H.JEBAT: And your mission is to take my head on a platter to your master, is that it?

H.TUAH: Exactly; and now that you have got the point, prepare to meet your destiny, Jebat.

H.JEBAT: (*Laughing*) Tuah, Tuah, my destiny, like yours and even that of the tyrant whom you serve is in the Hand of Almighty God, and no one can change it. It has all been willed, and if it is God's will that I shall die at the hand of my brother and dearest friend, then so be it. However, allow me at least to clear my mind. What is it that has thus turned you against me: me, whom you have always regarded as a piece of yourself, the very beat of your heart?

H.TUAH: You have been a rebel, Jebat, and there is only one punishment for rebellion against king and country. You know that as well as I do.

H.JEBAT: I used to believe that once, but no longer. I lost faith in those laws and principles when the tyrant decided to kill you. To me, human laws can have no meaning if they so blatantly contravene the laws of God, Tuah. Can't you see the blind fallacy in the laws by which Melaka is governed?

H.TUAH: The laws are immutable, Jebat; they have existed for as long as this noble land itself. They have only one aim: the protection of the Sultan, his dignity and his *daulat*. Our duty is to obey, not to question them.

H.JEBAT: Does nothing else matter?

H.TUAH: Nothing. Not even the Sultan's so-called injustice against me, for in calling me back he has forgiven me. My sins no longer exist, if there were any in the first place. The royal pardon has cleared them all.

H.JEBAT: How very convenient! Do you know the sultan's instructions were to have you killed and thrown into the river as meat for the crocodiles? And now, after somehow having avoided, thanks to the disobedience of the *bendahara*, the very laws and principles you so highly extol you come here to tell me how sacred they are. Isn't that somewhat ironic?

H.TUAH: My life was saved by destiny, Jebat. No human power can control the laws of destiny.

H.JEBAT: And true friendship and affection—do these things mean nothing? Perhaps you do not realize that everything—the insults I cast upon the tyrant, my so-called rebellion, my occupying this palace—all, all of this was done for you, Tuah, friend and brother, as a means of taking revenge against the sultan on your behalf. And now you come back from the dead, as it were, to accuse me of disloyalty.

H.TUAH: I am thankful to you for your affection. I have always valued it; will cherish it as long as I live. But no matter what justification you give, your treason remains unpardonable. It will be remembered in history as much as will be our mutual love and friendship. Generations will debate the issue, and each will imbue its own colouring. The unfortunate fact is that, at this point in history, your deed are considered treasonous and deserving of death; that I am fated to cause your death.

H.JEBAT: And what will history say to how personal devotion, all sacred ties of love between sworn brothers are here inhumanly cut by you in the name of loyalty to a tyrant?

H.TUAH: It's a question of priorities, Jebat. I did love you once and still do. But things have changed, the circumstances are different. I have to choose between you and my master. It has been very difficult, believe me. I have spent sleepless nights debating with myself.

H.JEBAT: The sultan who unjustly sentenced you to death not once but twice, to him you give your devotion. I don't understand it at all, Tuah.

H.TUAH: I redeemed myself, Jebat.

H.JEBAT: Yes, by supplying him with the helpless Tun Teja to satisfy his lust and now, this time, by agreeing to kill your life-long companion and brother. (*Hang Tuah remains silent*). By the way, you still have not told me how you managed to escape death.

H.TUAH: That's a long story to be recounted by future parents to their children after dinner as they sit on the landings of their *kampung* houses . . . But let's not change the subject, Jebat. As I have told you, it's a question of inconstant circumstances.

H.JEBAT: And shifting loyalties at the mere altering of the wind. Or is it a few more acres of land, an additional medal or two for your ample chest?

H.TUAH: That's unfair. You are still in my heart, my friend. None will be sorrier to see you die today, should it turn out that way.

H.JEBAT: But Tuah . . .

H.TUAH: Enough! I came with a mission and I must complete it. Much time has been wasted. Prepare to meet your end, Jebat. The crowd is getting restless. Their impatience will soon tear down the palace gates unless this matter is settled one way or another.

H.JEBAT: The unruly changeable rabble; as unpredictable as ever. Do you value their affections so much?

H.TUAH: I believe you did so too once, not so very long ago.

H.JEBAT: But I learnt my lesson as, no doubt, one bitter day you will too when the absurdity of the fate

we are making for ourselves dawns upon you. It
is time to remember . . .

H.TUAH: Time, yes time breeds many changes, and time
waits for no one, not even one as great as you,
Jebat, for now your time has come. Prove that
you can fight as well as you can talk.

*Drums, a loud scream. An elegant silat fight begins, and deceived by
Hang Tuah, Jebat is wounded with the keris, Taming Sari.*

H.JEBAT: Treacherous, treacherous! Oh Tuah, Hang Tuah,
I die, I die. I did not believe you were capable of
deceit, of stabbing below the belt, of violating the
sacred laws of combat.

H.TUAH: As if you did not know . . . everything is
permitted in love and war. It's an old dictum . . .
my friend. Besides, Taming Sari belongs to me,
Jebat, remember.

H.JEBAT: Alas, I die! Take my greetings to your family,
Tuah. I forgive your trespass, and may God
pardon you this deed. My soul I commit to
God, consign my mortal remains to you. Give
me a proper burial. This is my last wish friend,
brother, more than brother.

*Hang Jebat dies. There is a great deal of commotion. The ladies
scream, as everyone gets close to Hang Jebat's Jebat's body. Hang
Tuah violently throws away his keris, and kneels on the stage-floor.
He throws away his keris, his hands cover his face for a moment
or two; and the move to his nose; he hands as he does a salutation
(sembah).*

H.TUAH: *Inna lillahi wa inna ilaihi rajiun.* To God we belong and to God we all return. Goodbye, my dear brother.

Hang Tuah, in a state of shock, continues to kneel near Hang Jebat's body. He begins to sob uncontrollably. Several pall-bearers enter and Hang Jebat's body is carried in procession around the acting area and then off-stage. Hang Tuah's face is still covered by his hands. The single spotlight on him, which gradually fades out.

SCENE 7

The Announcer enters, as before, with a spotlight only on his face.
His words are also displayed on a signboard.

ANNOUNCER: Hang Tuah, in the name and form of Maharaja
Lela, a Perak chieftain, is charged with the
murder of James W. W. Birch, the British
Resident of Perak on November the 1st 1875. He
pleads not guilty.

The Court-house as before. The judges enter and take their seats,
Hang Tuah is in the witness box.

JUDGE 1:   Read the charges, bailiff.

BAILIFF: The charge is as follows: That in the year
1875, you, Hang Tuah, in the name and shape
of Maharaja Lela, conspired with other Malay
officials in Perak to murder the Honourable Mr
J.W.W. Birch, British Resident in that State, and
that you, as ring leader, knowingly, and willingly
effected the foul deed in Pasir Salak on or about
the 1st day of November 1875 by piercing a
spear through the palm-leaf walls of a riverside
bath-house.

JUDGE 1:   Do you or do you not admit having committed
the murder?

H.TUAH:	I do, Your Honour, but I do not consider it murder.
JUDGE 1:	Does that mean you plead guilty to the charge as read?
H.TUAH:	No, Your Honour, I do not.
JUDGE 3:	What is the meaning of this equivocation? You say that you did commit the murder and yet maintain you are not guilty. How do you reconcile those two blatantly contradictory stands?
H.TUAH:	It's like this, Your Honour. The deed can be considered a crime or a blessing, depending on which point of view is adopted.
JUDGE 3:	Meaning?
H.TUAH:	If we look at the deed as a true Malaysian should, and particularly one of my race . . .
JUDGE 3:	A proto-Malay?
H.TUAH:	I know Winstedt called me proto-Malay, but such derogatory terms are never used these days, Your Honour, except by Western anthropologists. I mean the Bumiputera, and the Melayu. So to backtrack a little, if the killing of the British gentleman is seen from a native perspective, it becomes praise-worthy, one deserving of celebration and a good pension for the living descendants of Maharaja Lela, who carved for himself a niche in Malay history by gloriously sacrificing his own life. He was

defending Malay political and territorial rights, the freedom of the Malays to practice their own religion, observe their own customs and conduct their own administration in their own manner . . .

JUDGE 1: Just a point of clarification—was there, at that time, any organized administration in Perak? Historians tell us that numerous chiefs and opportunities had carved out for themselves their own little kingdoms at river mouths and other strategic places, built stockades, and then attempted through coercion, terrorism, and other unorthodox means to extract taxes from those who happened to pass, using gangsters whom they euphemistically named warriors. Wasn't that the case?

H.TUAH: Although there may be some truth in all of that, it is essentially a foreign point of view, meant to leave the impression that the orang Melayu were barbarians incapable of ruling themselves, that British intervention was a God-given blessing. It happened in various ways all over the world, including Melaka. But, Your Honour, one just has to take a glance at the glory of Melaka. You will find there a fine example of a kingdom ruled by Malays, of course with the co-operation of many races.

JUDGE 2: From what I know there were many Indians and Arabs in the high ranks of the Melaka, administration. Was that true?

H.TUAH: Yes, Your Honour.

JUDGE 2:   You were saying something about the point of view; remember, Birch's brutal killing . . .

H.TUAH: Ah yes, Your Honour. I got carried away—it seems inevitable when one talks of medieval Melaka. I apologize for the digression. You see, Your Honour, if the British point of view is taken, then, without any question at all, I become the murderer of that late English gentleman.

JUDGE 3:   But murder *was* committed, was it not?

H.TUAH: No, Your Honour, I beg to differ. A killing did take place, but no murder was committed.

JUDGE 3:   Really? How's that possible?

H.TUAH: When one kills a colonizer, who by definition is essentially a blood-sucker, and saves his people, that cannot be considered a murder, Your Honour. Otherwise, every member of the security forces upon whose shoulders lies the noble responsibility of defending his nation becomes a potential mass murderer. Thus too, not Hitler alone, despite his notoriety, but every military leader, every administrator who deals with defense, and internal security, even every surgeon who loses a patient becomes a murderer. In the light of all this, the killing of J.W.W. Birch, which I as Maharaja Lela proudly admit having been responsible for, must be considered a heroic act! It must be highlighted in the history of our land . . .

JUDGE 2:   Tell us what caused you to kill the British Resident and how it happened.

H.TUAH: You see, Your Honour, Birch as Resident
            of Perak was insensitive to Malay feelings.
            He could neither understand nor speak our
            language, Bahasa Melayu, and so could not
            communicate with the people. He had no
            worthwhile knowledge of local traditions and
            customs, and did not appreciate them; on the
            contrary, contrasting our behaviour with those
            of the British, he insolently regarded us Melayu
            as barbaric people. On the whole, his high-
            handed actions aroused hostility. But his most
            serious mistake was his attempt to overthrow
            the established political structures, to pit Raja
            Yusuf against Raja Abdullah, in the usual British
            manner of divide and rule. The princes saw
            through Birch's scheme, and so together with
            me, and a host of others decided to eliminate
            him, for the sake of Malay unity and to preserve
            our cherished customs and manners. So his
            death was carefully planned, and extremely well
            executed. We believe it was fated, Your Honour,
            for at a spirit séance, locally known as a *berhantu*
            ceremony, held some time before the actual
            event, foretold a white man's death.

JUDGE 2:   Does the *berhantu* thing mean that your men
            were in league with the devil?

H.TUAH: (*Laughing*) No, no, Your Honour. *Hantu* is just
            the old Malay word for spirit, not the devil who
            is called Shaitan. Actually, Shaitan is a figure
            imported with Islam. Before that, there were a
            whole range of Hindu gods and goddesses, called
            dewa and *dewi* respectively, as well as demons
            and giants, *bhuta*, *rakshasa* and so on.

JUDGE 3:   So the Malays were Hindus, like the Balinese. Is that what you are saying?

H.TUAH: (*Hesitantly*) I . . . I suppose some of them were. But I believe most of them were animists. Even to this day some of our *bomoh* and *pawang* work with spirits, some to help, others to harm. So we have black magic, *ilmu jahat*, and white magic.

JUDGE 1:   All this is really fascinating, but we must move on. Remember, this is a trial, not a lesson in anthropology or mythology, although the subject of *berhantu* did come in. Going back to your earlier statement, then, it can be surmised that you and a handful of others were directly responsible for the British Resident's death.

H.TUAH: I do not deny that courageous deed, Your Honour.

JUDGE 2:   What, in your opinion, would happen if everyone, like you, took the law into his own hands? Surely there would be chaos in the country.

H.TUAH: Possibly Your Honour, but I believe chaos caused by local persons to whom the country belongs is anytime preferable to chaos caused by intruding foreigners.

JUDGE 3:   I don't see how that makes any sense. Surely any kind of chaos would be negative and destructive.

JUDGE 1:   Hang Tuah, you are in fact advocating for yourself the very sins you have condemned in others like the late J.W.W. Birch. Isn't that the

71

case? What do you think will be the result if everyone took the law into his own hands, behaved in the manner you and your companion did on 1ˢᵗ November, 1875? Surely, some kind of control needs to be exerted, to restrain such people.

H.TUAH: Your Honour, that is an impossible proposition. They need leaders like me, with a clear head, and the ability to act swiftly and decisively. If this had not been done on that fateful November day, the Malay populace would have been driven in herds into slavery, while the British ironically claimed to be passing anti-slavery enactments. Some of us saw through the British ruse, and did what had to be done. In this case, the real criminal was J.W.W. Birch, Your Honour, not yours truly.

JUDGE 2: You seem altogether convinced that you managed to achieve a great deal by murdering a single individual, a human being like you, but in reality, a much higher British soul.

H.TUAH: Your Honour, it is not a question of a single death. In all of this, we are not concerned merely with that entity, J.W.W. Birch, whose bearded face sometimes stares at us from the pages of history books. It is not this or that particular individual that matters, but the symbol. Birch stood for colonial administration at its ignorant and disinterested worst. Thus, the colonizing power became in the eyes of the local population odious and evil, something to be got rid of, no matter how. Where many feared to tread, I ventured. I accomplished in one stroke what thousands of ordinary, docile members of my Melayu community could not. The sense of achievement was altogether too exhilarating for words, Your Honour, especially since the news spread all over the British Empire. Thus, I too became a symbol.

JUDGE 3: How incredible! What an imagination the man has!

H.TUAH: You see, Your Honour, when they needed a picture of mine to use on the new Bank Bumiputera building in Kuala Lumpur, no one knew what exactly I looked like. In those ancient Malacca days, photography was yet to be introduced. Numerous sketches and paintings that hung in the grand palace were burnt down with the palace itself, others were lost over the centuries. So, they created a rather unflattering image to represent me, Your Honour. There are examples right here, in the lobby of this theatre. Let me state categorically that the clash between J.W.W. Birch and Maharaja Lela was a clash of cultures and symbols, not personalities. I believe as individuals both of us could be amiable, perhaps even to a fault.

JUDGE 2: How very informative! How come it is not recorded anywhere, Hang Tuah, that you were also a fine orator?

H.TUAH: Thank you, Your Honour—just one of my many minor achievements, neglected by historians in favour of dates, political events, and upheavals, wars, coronations and occasional scandals. Such omission is quite common, you will agree with me, no doubt. The fine art of oratory died out in ancient Greece and Rome; today, it is little appreciated. Why, even our lawyers merely mumble meaningless sounds which they expect their listeners to regard as words. Alas Cicero, if only you were alive!

JUDGE 1: That was a fine oratorical exercise, perhaps a welcome digression too. But Hang Tuah, can we address ourselves to the subject at hand, the charge you are supposed to be answering? Does all this mean that you claim innocence? I know it is somewhere in there, in that large and undoubtedly impressive outpouring of words, phrases, interminable sentences.

H.TUAH: I believe so, Your Honour.

JUDGE 1: I do hope the members of this learned assembly have been able to follow the defendant's amusing, yet erudite discourse. We should take a short break here.

BAILIFF: *Bangun*!

The judges exit, followed by Hang Tuah. Lights dim and fade out.

SCENE 8

Words on a signboard:

Datuk Hang Tuah meets a Taiwanese tycoon, George Tan, and his niece to settle a long outstanding matter. Then follows his meeting with Encik Rahim, a local Malay businessman who has to come up with a possible deal with a Korean firm. Finally, Hang Tuah's office is visited by a representative of the people, claiming that Hang Tuah has in fact failed the Malays in many different ways.

Hang Tuah is in his office. A buzzer sounds, his secretary, Lena, enters. She is a pretty girl in her early twenties and is fashionably dressed.in sarung-kebaya.

H.TUAH: Enter.

LENA: Sorry to disturb you, Datuk.

H.TUAH: It's okay, my dear; no need to apologize. It's always a pleasure to see you. You know you are so beautiful.

LENA: Thank you, Datuk. Mr. George Tan is here to see you, Datuk.

H.TUAH: Send him in, send him in. (*The Secretary is about to leave*). And . . .

LENA: Datuk?

H.TUAH: Lena. Can I have the pleasure of your company this evening? You know I have been asking you for so long . . .

LENA: I'm sorry, Datuk. I am engaged tonight.

H.TUAH: Engaged again? You keep a busy schedule, don't you?

LENA: Yes, Datuk. Sorry. (*She walks out.*)

H.TUAH: Well, perhaps some other time then, Lena. But it had better be soon.

The buzzer sounds again. Enter George Tan with a very pretty young lady in a tight-fitting cheongsam. He's about fifty. She is in her early twenties.

G.TAN: Ah, good morning, Datuk.

H.TUAH: George, how nice to see you again! How are you today? (*Shaking his hand*) And this . . .

G.TAN: Fine, Datuk, Ah. This . . . this is Felicia, my niece, Datuk, from Taiwan. She just arrived last night.

H.TUAH: Ah, Felicia (*Shaking her hand*), how do you do?

FELICIA: Thank you, Datuk, I am fine.

G.TAN: I have told her so much about you, she was very keen to meet you personally, Datuk. She is a fashion model and a minor film star in Taiwan.

H.TUAH: Ah, really?

FELICIA: Just a minor one, Datuk.

H.TUAH: Film star, ha? How interesting. Just visiting Malaysia, Felicia?

FELICIA: Yes, just a short visit. A couple of weeks, perhaps a little longer. Depends.

H.TUAH: Depends upon what? Are you shooting a film in this country or do you have some other business?

FELICIA: No business, Datuk.

H.TUAH: Ah, pleasure, then. (*Laughs and holds her hand again. Felicia does not resist.*)

G.TAN: Perhaps we should talk business first, Datuk, and then . . .

H.TUAH: I see, I see. Business before pleasure, huh? (*Guides Felicia to a seat.*) Sit down, sit down, my dear. (*They all sit*). Yes, what can I do for you, my friend Henry?

G.TAN: Not Henry, Datuk; George, George Tan.

H.TUAH: Oh, sorry, George Tan. You know, in this business, I meet so many people. My sincere apologies.

G.TAN: It's okay, Datuk, just a minor slip of the mouth, I mean the tongue. You see, Datuk, it's about the contract for the supply of those barges . . .

H.TUAH: The barges . . . barges. Oh yes, I remember. (*Draws Felicia close to him*). The barges . . .

G.TAN: My partners in Taiwan are getting a little impatient, Datuk. They cannot confirm other contracts until . . .

H.TUAH: Yes, yes. I understand. It shouldn't take too long now. You see, Henry, I mean George, the preliminary discussions have already been held among all parties but the Board has yet to make a final decision. I have, however, managed to get your tender into the shortlist.

G.TAN: Thank you, Datuk, that's very kind of you.

H.TUAH: You see, there are two other really good tenders; one perhaps even more attractive than yours, in terms of prices, I mean. The difference is quite substantial, you know, and so I really cannot push yours too hard, just in case . . . however . . . the 10% commission.

G.TAN: Perhaps I can get my partners in Taiwan to increase it a little . . . say up to 15%. And, as we discussed previously, the money, it need not come here at all . . . it can be arranged, quite easily, Datuk.

H.TUAH: Thank you for being so understanding. Alright, I will talk to the members of the Board.

G.TAN: Since you are the Chairman, perhaps the others will just go along with your recommendation. After all they don't have to be given precise details.

H.TUAH: As I said, I can only try.

G.TAN: By the way, Datuk. I have also received instructions to offer you a return trip to Taipei—all expenses paid—in case you wish to have specific follow up discussions with my partners. Of course, that will only be possible once they are sure . . .

H.TUAH: All expenses paid, did you say?

G.TAN: That's right, Datuk.

H.TUAH: That should help. You see every little bit counts. There's a Malay saying *sedikit-sedikit lama-lama menjadi bukit.* You understand what that means, I suppose, Felicia?

FELICIA: No. I'm sorry, I don't understand Malaysian at all, Datuk.

H.TUAH: Perhaps, this is your first time in Malaysia, then. There is no such thing as a Malaysian language. This is a saying in the language of the Malays. It means little, little, become hill.

FELICIA: I get it. What a cute expression!

H.TUAH: I think there should be no problem, George. I *will* persuade the Board. Just give me a little more time; perhaps after the Taiwan trip. Felicia, when I am in Taiwan perhaps I could have the pleasure of your company? (*Felicia merely smiles.*)

G.TAN: O, thank you, Datuk, thank you very much! I really appreciate that. I knew I could count on you.

H.TUAH: And now to more pleasant things. I mean the pleasure following the business. (*All laugh*) Will you have a drink? A brandy or something. And for you Felicia, perhaps some coffee, tea, or me? (*Laughs*)

G.TAN: It's alright, Datuk. We have taken too much of your time already. We really have to move on. But if you have time, we can meet this evening for Chinese dinner, perhaps at the Golden Phoenix, say at about 8.00pm? I will reserve a private room.

H.TUAH: The three of us?

G.TAN: The three of us; but I will have to run away quickly. I have another appointment at 9.00. You and Felicia can stay on, and if you don't mind, Datuk, you can drop her home later on.

H.TUAH: That should be quite interesting. Don't you agree, Felicia? We can talk about Taiwan among other things. I don't think have ever met a real film star before. Yes, George that sounds great. Is there any curfew hour for you, Felicia?

FELICIA: (*Laughs*) Curfew hour? I am not sure what you mean, Datuk? I am sorry.

G.TAN: No such thing, Datuk. (*Laughing*) She's a grown up girl. Thank you very much for your time, and for agreeing . . .

H.TUAH: Oh, it's only a small matter.

George Tan moves on ahead. Hang Tuah puts his hand around Felicia's waist, gradually leading her towards the door.

H.TUAH: Until tonight then, Felicia.

(Hang Tuah tries to embrace her; she breaks away, and follows George Tan out of Hang Tuah's office. Hang Tuah is alone) Yes, tonight. *(Sings)* Tonight . . . tonight . . .

Lights dim out, and when they come on again, Hang Tuah is at his desk as before. The buzzer sounds, and his Secretary enters.

H.TUAH: Enter.

LENA: Sorry to disturb you, Datuk.

H.TUAH: It's okay, my dear, Lena, no need to apologise. As I have said countless times before, it's always a pleasure to see you. You know you are so beautiful.

LENA: Thank you, Datuk. Encik Rahim Long to see you, Datuk.

H.TUAH: Please send him in. *(The Secretary is about to leave)*. And . . . Lena, can I . . .

LENA: I'm sorry, Datuk. I am engaged tonight. *(She walks out quickly.)*

H.TUAH: *(To himself)* Well, perhaps some other time then, Lena.

The buzzer sounds, and Encik Rahim Long enters.

H.TUAH: Hello, Rahim! Long time no see! Come in, come in *(They shake hands)*. What brings you here, my friend?

RAHIM: (*Taking a seat*). You see Datuk Hang Tuah, it's like this . . .

H.TUAH: Yes, go on, I am listening.

RAHIM: I have just been offered a large share in a joint-venture factory, Datuk.

H.TUAH: Congratulations! With whom?

RAHIM: A Korean firm, Datuk. I was wondering if you would be interested in coming in.

H.TUAH: You are offering to take me in as a partner—do I understand you correctly?

RAHIM: Yes, Datuk. You see the amount involved is very large. I don't have that much capital. So I thought I'd invite you to join me.

H.TUAH: I see. How much is involved?

RAHIM: 500 million. You put in half and I can raise the other half. Together, we will control 51%. You can be Chairman of the company.

H.TUAH: 250 million?

RAHIM: You see, Datuk, besides the capital, your presence on the Board as Chairman will also bring tremendous prestige, with your connections and reputation . . .

H.TUAH: And what's the expected profit?

RAHIM: First year, not much. After that things should improve, perhaps 20-25%. You should be able to recover everything in about five to six years. That's not a bad deal.

H.TUAH: Certainly sounds tempting.

RAHIM: I have the details here in this proposal paper. You can keep this copy and examine it at leisure.

H.TUAH: Alright. How much time do I have to give you an answer?

RAHIM: I'm afraid not much. I have to send a fax message to Korea and confirm acceptance within a fortnight. There's another party interested. Somehow through some connections in Korea, I managed to get the offer before others.

H.TUAH: Okay, let me think about it for a couple of days. You see, I may not be able to put the shares in my own name. You know, sometimes being a VIP too can be a problem.

RAHIM: But the advantages are certainly far greater, I am sure, Datuk.

H.TUAH: No doubt about that, my friend. No doubt at all. Consider it done. You see the amount involved is huge, and with all the recent actions of the Anti-Corruption Agency . . . I will find some way.

RAHIM: Thank you! Thank you very much Datuk! I knew I could count on you! And the ACA . . . They won't touch anyone like you, Datuk, I am sure of that.

H.TUAH: These are great times for people like us, Rahim.

RAHIM: I agree with you Datuk. We never had it so good. We have to thank May 13 for all this, Datuk. How could people like us afford to buy cars, bungalows and so on only a quarter of a century ago? Today, I believe we have more millionaires even than the Chinese, without actually struggling like them.

H.TUAH: True, true. Still, one has to be careful. One never knows, with so much of greed and jealousy around.

RAHIM: Looks as if it's settled, then. I am glad it worked out. There would have been no problem at all getting an Ali-Baba arrangement, but I thought its best to keep it in Bumi hands, and so I came to you.

H.TUAH: That's wise. That way we can maximize the opportunities available to us, make use of all the favourable policies, while we still have them.

RAHIM: Well, Datuk, thank you very much for the conformation of the partnership. I will immediately inform the Koreans, and we'll take it from there. (*Leaving*)

H.TUAH: Hey, have a drink; some brandy . . . or something; to celebrate.

RAHIM: Got to go, Datuk. Some other time, perhaps.

They shake hands and Rahim leaves. Lights dim, and black out. When they come on again, Hang Tuah is as before at his desk. The buzzer sounds, and Lena, Hang Tuah's secretary, enters.

H.TUAH: Enter.

LENA: Sorry to disturb you, Datuk.

H.TUAH: It's okay, my dear; no need to apologise . . .

LENA: (*Cutting him short*) There's someone to see you, Datuk.

H.TUAH: I am not expecting anyone else. Who is it this time?

LENA: He does not want to give me his name. Seems to be really impatient to come in.

H.TUAH: What does he want?

LENA: He will not tell me. He insists on seeing you personally at once.

H.TUAH: That sounds a little fishy. Call my bodyguards.

LENA: They are nowhere to be seen, Datuk. Perhaps, they have gone for their coffee break. Can I send him in? This stranger?

H.TUAH: Okay, send him in; but also send for my bodyguards, immediately.

LENA: Yes, Datuk. (*Leaving*)

H.TUAH: And . . .

LENA:	Sorry, Datuk, I am engaged tonight. (*She walks out quickly*).
H.TUAH:	(*To himself*) You certainly keep a busy schedule, Lena.

Man 3 enters; he is a little rugged but on the whole well-mannered.

MAN 3:	I thought you were not going to see me at all.
H.TUAH:	Who are you?
MAN 3:	It does not matter. I have come here to make certain requests.
H.TUAH:	Requests?
MAN 3:	Yes.
H.TUAH:	What kind of requests . . . or is it demands?
MAN 3:	It's all the same.
H.TUAH:	Are you from the PLO or the Khalistan Liberation Army?
MAN 3:	Very funny. Do I look like a Palestinian or a Bengali Sikh?
H.TUAH:	Just a guess. Then tell me who you are. What do you want from me?
MAN 3:	It does not matter. Can I sit down?
H.TUAH:	Sure. Be my guest.

MAN 3:   (*Sitting down, and placing a pistol on the table*)
             Now, remember Hang Tuah—sorry, *Datuk*
             Hang Tuah—anything funny, and your brains
             will be blown to smithereens.

H.TUAH: You certainly sound very angry, young man.
             What is it you want? Come here to my place and
             make threats against me without even telling me
             what all this is about? In my day . . .

MAN 3:   First, let me tell you I represent the people, a
             great many people out there.

H.TUAH: Are you a State Assemblyman?

MAN 3:   Very funny. No.

H.TUAH: A Member of Parliament, then. You must know
             Karpal Singh.

MAN 3:   Now listen very carefully. We intend to punish
             the higher ups who are guilty.

H.TUAH: Guilty? Of what?

MAN 3:   Of corruption, of deceiving the people, by taking
             for themselves all the benefits accruing from the
             New Economic Policy and so on. The parasites.

(*He retrieves his pistol and places it in the pocket of his trousers.*)

H.TUAH: I don't understand.

MAN 3:   You don't, do you? Just let me tell you this. You
             and others like you have become filthy rich and
             fat on the bribery, the corruption, the cronyism,

the friendship with powerful ones, while the majority of us have not been able to get anything out of the NEP and other such schemes.

H.TUAH: I see. Didn't you buy any Amanah Saham Bumiputera shares?

MAN 3: Yes; a couple of hundred. But that won't make me rich.

H.TUAH: There's an old Malay saying, *sedikit-sedikit lama-lama* . . .

MAN 3: Oh, shut up!

H.TUAH: So you are here to redress the economic situation, I suppose; to get some contribution for your fund?

MAN 3: I did not come here to beg. I am to take from the rich to give to the poor, like Robin Hood and Hang Jebat.

H.TUAH: Jebat? You mean the man I killed?

MAN 3: Yes.

H.TUAH: He was no friend of the poor. Can you give me one instance of what he did for the poor? No, you can't. *I* was the hero, if you remember. That is why the *hikayat* is named after me, and not after that rebel and traitor, Jebat.

MAN 3: Did *you* do anything for the masses?

H.TUAH: Perhaps not much. But that was not my intention. You see, those were times quite different from the present, Encik . . . what's your name, by the way?

MAN 3:   It doesn't matter. I am not an individual. I am a symbol.

H.TUAH: Symbol? How interesting. What sort of symbol, if I may ask? You see, I too am supposed to be a symbol.

MAN 3:   I stand for the masses out there in the sun and the rain—they have remained poor and hungry since the days of the Melaka sultanate, perhaps even since, the Melayu people first came into being.

H.TUAH: The Melaka Sultanate! Ah, my favourite subject. I keep telling people all the time that those were great times. There has never been a place more glorious than Melaka.

MAN 3:   Glorious?

H.TUAH: Yes. It's all in *Sejarah Melayu*, and the *hikayat* named after me.

MAN 3:   A mere deception; a delusion.

H.TUAH: Deception? Delusion? How can you say that?

MAN 3:   A small circle of the raja's cronies got fat upon the wealth derived from the rich Chinese, Gujerati, Arab, Indonesian, and Parsi merchants. What did people like me get out of all that? Nothing.

H.TUAH: But there were other glories! The art and culture, the architecture, and so on.

MAN 3:   Mere appendages to lasciviousness. Can music and dancing fill the stomach—yes, perhaps if you are professional musicians, ballet dancers or university lecturers specializing in the performing arts. But how many such people does society need? As for the wealth of mediaeval Melaka—it was totally appropriated by the big shots.

H.TUAH: That can't be entirely true. Something did trickle down, I am certain, as it does even to this day . . . You see, I just increased the salaries of my driver and my Indonesian maids.

MAN 3:   Yes, the spillover. That's all we deserve, after people like you have fattened on the best.

H.TUAH: Too bad, but that's always been the reality; that's the way the world is made, my friend.

MAN 3:   So you admit the NEP was intended primarily for the rich to get richer?

H.TUAH: That was inevitable; perhaps a vicious cycle. The opportunities were all there, but to start with, there had to be some money. Money makes more money. It's an old principle confirmed by outstanding economists. If you don't have any to start with, it's just too bad. You should be happy your fellow Malays have struck it rich after all those years of British colonial administration and exploitation.

MAN 3:   In those days of your glorious Melaka, was it not the same then?

H.TUAH: O Melaka, my glorious Melaka! Yes, yes it was the same then, I must admit. I am afraid the poor will have to find other ways of getting rich.

MAN 3:   Other ways? You don't expect us to rob banks or murder the rich and abscond with their wealth, do you?

H.TUAH: No, I did not have that in mind, actually.

MAN 3:   Then what exactly *did* you have in mind? Tell me, tell me Hang Tuah, you who for the past five centuries have been mistakenly adored by the ordinary man as a hero? Tell me!

H.TUAH: Well, you see. It's like this. How shall I put it?

MAN 3:   You are just like the others—opportunists. You prefer to deal with those of other races, even foreigners, because they make you rich; they provide you with fringe benefits. What can the poor of your own kind do for you? Nothing. You come to us when you need the favours from us. Then you seduce us with little gifts, wild promises intended never to materialize—all part of your evil scheme to advance yourself. Do you know that over the past three decades the number of the poor has actually increased?

H.TUAH: Perhaps, with the population increase. But percentages. See the percentages.

MAN 3:   I do not understand percentages, Hang Tuah. I only hear the cry of my hungry children, the groaning of my equally hungry stomach, and I see around me the monstrous factories belching black smoke, darkening the skies; I see the massive houses, bigger and more fashionable cars, all owned by people like you. There was nothing for me in your golden Melaka, and there still is nothing for me in this new era—once described as the glorious and potential future— yes not too long ago, in the mid-eighties. There's nothing for me and the likes of me, Hero of this and Hero of that. I am surprised that some people think of you as the Robin Hood of Malacca.

H.TUAH: I thought they gave that title to Jebat. Apparently, according to some pf our local playwrights, he represents the masses, while I represent feudal ideals.

MAN 3:   What is the difference? Neither Jebat nor you have done anything for us; and we like fools have been idolizing you.

LENA: (*Rushing in*) Datuk, the crowds are becoming unmanageable. They are screaming, pushing into the building.

H.TUAH: I told you to call my bodyguards! Call the police! Or the army if necessary!

MAN 3:   It's no use. The telephone lines have been cut; your building has been surrounded.

LENA: Oh no . . . (*faints*)

H.TUAH: Telephone lines cut? Wisma Hang Tuah
               surrounded? Have you no more respect for me?
               Remember, I am still the hero . . . what is this? A
               revolution?

MAN 3:   No revolution, Hang Tuah. Merely a turn of the
               tide; the voice of the oppressed. Perhaps you will
               run amuck again, as once you did in Majapahit,
               as Jebat did in Melaka, Taming Sari buried in his
               flesh. That made him braver than ever . . . run
               smack, kill a few hundred once again. Increase
               your stature as a hero. After all, life never really
               had any value to you, did it, Hang Tuah? I mean
               real, ordinary, everyday life.

H.TUAH: What need is there for such insane behaviour?

MAN 3:   I have told you my needs and theirs. They have
               come to test you, to see if you are really a hero.

H.TUAH: But I still am. Just go and read my adventures,
               ask around. I am still remembered for my
               outstanding services to the Sultan of Melaka.

MAN 3:   You live in a dream—The sultan of Melaka; the
               glorious days of mediaeval Melaka. That Melaka
               has been long been dead and gone. Hang Tuah
               for you time seems to have stopped. It stops
               when it is convenient, when you do not wish to
               come face to face with common everyday reality.
               Psychiatrists have a term for it, which I do not at
               present recall . . . some kind of selective amnesia.
               You perpetuate your dreams, switch off your
               mental computers except when it suits you.

The crowds burst onto the stage. They are carrying placards and signs emblazoned with various expressions, some saying "Down with Hang Tuah"; others supporting him with slogans like "Hang Tuah, our great hero". In the end, they surround him, demand that he be tried in the Sasaran Court. They carry him over their heads in procession chanting. "Death to Hang Tuah!" "Death to Hang Tuah!". "To the Sasaran Court!". "To the Sasaran Court!". "Death to Hang Tuah!".

H.TUAH: Patience; patience, gentlemen. I should be garlanded and carried in triumph, not manhandled rudely in this manner! What has come upon you, you rowdy rabble of Melaka? Remember, I am still the hero, even if you don't think so. History will remember me as such. Where are you taking me? Where?

MAN 3:   To the Sasaran Court. Let the people decide if you are a hero or a villain, Hang Tuah.

H.TUAH: The Sasaran Court? What craziness! That's no place for a hero like me. Do you think all this cruelty on your part is some sort of theatre? Let me go, or I'll be forced to call my bodyguards! The police! The army! Ridiculous!

MAN 3:   Let the court decide, Once and for all, whether you are a hero or villain.

H.TUAH: History will never forgive you for this. Help! Help!

SCENE 9

The Sasaran Court. The words said by the Announcer are also boldly displayed on sign. Hang Tuah is in the witness stand.

ANNOUNCER: Hang Tuah is charged with causing the May 13 riots in Kuala Lumpur in the year 1969; with the subversion of the New Economic Policy, as well as succeeding policies; negligence of his ardent admirers, whom he has let down very badly. He is also charged with being involved in bribery, corruption, and other allied crimes against the country, the Malay race, and their religion.

JUDGE 1: Bailiff, please read the charges.

BAILIFF: Hang Tuah, you are hereby charged with the following crimes: Causing the May 13 riots in Kuala Lumpur in the year 1969; with the subversion of the New Economic Policy, as well as succeeding policies; negligence of your ardent admirers, whom you have let down very badly. You are also charged with being involved in bribery, corruption, and other allied crimes against our beloved Malaysia, and against your race and religion.

JUDGE 2: How do you plead, Hang Tuah?

H.TUAH: Your Honour, the charges are ridiculous. I am not guilty. I have not let anyone down. I am still the hero who has captured their imagination and retained their admiration. I have fired their dreams for several centuries. In fact, if anything, I have become even more of a hero since 1969.

JUDGE 1:   Are you saying then that you are not guilty of any of the crimes mentioned by the bailiff a moment ago?

H.TUAH: I am not guilty, Your Honour.

JUDGE 2:   Do you know that as a result of the May 13 1969 riots, hundreds of people were killed, thousands of others lost their property? The fires are still smouldering in their hearts.

H.TUAH: That was inevitable, Your Honour. A small price to pay for an immense gain.

JUDGE 3:   Gain, did you say?

H.TUAH: Gain, Your Honour. You see, as a result of the 1969 incident, there has developed greater patriotism, an unprecedented sense of nationalism. True independence came only in 1969.

JUDGE 1:   How so? Every child knows we gained independence in 1957 as the Federation of Malaya, and again in 1965 with the formation of Malaysia.

H.TUAH: In name only, Your Honour. Real independence only came in 1969.

JUDGE 2:   Would you care to elaborate?

H.TUAH: With pleasure. You see, Your Honour, even though the British left in 1957, we were still mentally colonized; for one thing, we still used the English language, with Bahasa Melayu being relegated to village schools and *sekolah pondok*. The country was still backward. It was only after 1969 that we began, for the first time, to develop our country along lines which gave every race and every person a place in the sun, without racial prejudice or bias. And, of course, there are the countless monuments, such as the Kuala Lumpur City Centre, and the Kuala Lumpur International Airport, the Penang Bridge, that have made the country justly famous.

JUDGE 1:   Most of them built by foreigners, funded by them, and belonging to them.

H.TUAH.   I agree, Your Honour. But that is only a temporary measure, the Ali-Baba arrangement, pardon me, I mean the joint-venture thing, Your Honour. In time, it will no longer be necessary; the Malaysians, and especially the Malays will take over.

JUDGE 1:   Many will not agree with your interpretation, Hang Tuah. Do you realize this?

H.TUAH: Yes, Your Honour. Any statement discussing matters such as racial imbalance is bound to be taken one way by some, and another way by others. That is only natural. There can be no concurrence. Some will feel deprived of necessity. But I believe the deprivation was only temporary,

97

a necessary evil. Now that the NEP has been over since 1990, with its objectives achieved, there is no need for the protective measure instituted at the beginning of the NEP period. That should satisfy everyone and lead to greater tolerance, understanding and harmony.

JUDGE 3: But the NEP under new names and guises has been continued. It is still going on. Some say it will go on indefinitely. What do you say to that?

H.TUAH: I don't believe that is entirely true. Yes, some extension has certainly taken place, because the Malays were slow to catch up: they needed more time. But I stress that this is only temporary.

JUDGE 2: Some people, especially the Malays, believe temporary means forever.

H.TUAH: That is merely because their language is poor, Your Honour. Malay is still a developing language like mediaeval English. You see, all the agreements have been written in English, and most of the discussion also takes place in that foreign language. Naturally, such confusion is to be expected, Your Honour, as even Google translations are often imprecise or inaccurate. As they all get educated and acquire university degrees, hopefully up to PhD level, their language too will improve.

JUDGE 3: Would you say that everyone in this country is at last equal?

H.TUAH: No, Your Honour. There can never be such a thing as absolute equality. No two persons are created absolutely alike, and completely equal. That's one of the great divine mysteries, Your Honour. It's said that out of the billions who walk this earth, no two persons' fingerprints are exactly alike. This is also the case with their DNA. There is no need to elaborate, Your Honour. It will only lead to religious controversies, and philosophical discourses few in this theatre are prepared to follow, especially at this late hour. I can already see them yawning from boredom, Your Honour.

JUDGE 1:   Would you say too, that due to unequal conditions—social, political, economic, and other factors—the chances are not available for absolute equality?

H.TUAH: That is inevitable, Your Honour.

JUDGE 2:   Inevitable?

H.TUAH: Yes, Your Honour. There are many things that make up the machinery of administration, the most important being people. Thus, the machinery of administration functions according to the level of efficiency of people operating it. Individuals may be influenced by their inherent weaknesses or by their deliberate choice. Thus, the machinery's efficiency is bound to be affected.

JUDGE 1:   Are you suggesting inefficiency and self-interest as possible factors that undermine the running of the machinery?

H.TUAH: Yes, Your Honour.

JUDGE 1:   Suppose it is put to you that you too, as a cog in the machine of administration, were motivated by self-interest. Would that not be a true and accurate description of your conduct and character?

H.TUAH: I refuse to answer that, Your Honour.

JUDGE 2:   Suppose it is further put to you that your refusal to answer is an admission of your guilt?

H.TUAH: I have nothing further to say, Your Honour. Let the jury decide if as a senior cog in the government machinery I have been motivated by self-interest or if, as a businessman, I have been guided solely by motives of profit without due consideration of human, moral, religious, or ethical values. Even if I do plead guilty, Your Honour, it is likely that not everyone present in this theatre today will believe me. Similarly, if I claim innocence, some will still continue to regard me as a completely foul being. The debate will almost certainly go on forever, as it has over the centuries.

JUDGE 1:   Is that your last statement on this matter?

H.TUAH: Perhaps just one more, with Your Honour's kind permission.

JUDGE 2:   Go on.

H.TUAH: I have lived a fruitful life since the day I was born 600 years or so ago, although, regretfully, historians have recently cast doubts on my very existence, taking me as a figment of some people's fertile imagination, and the Malacca government has decided, without even consulting me, that I am no longer immortal. Personally, I believe they are totally wrong. I certainly existed in the past, and will continue to do so for a long time in the future. As far as the present goes, as you can see for yourselves, Honourable judges, I am still very much alive. I certainly have no need to prove that. You may recall, Your Honours, that it was I who once said that the Malays can never be lost from this world: *tak akan Melayu hilang di dunia.* I may be whatever I am but without me, the Malays will have no real hero. And where does a community stand without a hero? What is a community worth without a hero? Nothing, Your Honours. No doubt as time passes, more and more opinions will be expressed about me, and all that I symbolize, for, as often mentioned during the present illegal and unnecessary trial, I am more than a person. I am, this court will recall, a symbol. I can only pray that the present jury of learned persons and future juries, who will undoubtedly examine me under their microscopes whether in courts such as this, in literature classes, or in theatres such as this, will remember that to a degree the roles we play on this world-stage are assigned to us by Destiny. No doubt we have a limited control over what we are or what we do, but there are also factors beyond our selves that direct our fate, limit our conduct. If I had been born at a different time and in a different clime, then my character, my behaviour, and all my actions, nay even my very skin colour, the shape of my nose, the colour of my eyes, my whole appearance would have been different. Such is the miracle of divine creation. To most Malays, particularly those who have not become too Westernized, I have been, and still am, a hero. To other societies, other nations, I mean very little, perhaps nothing, for it is very likely that they have not even heard of me. Thus, fame is circumstantial, and so are our deeds. "There is a Destiny that shapes our ends", so said Hamlet, "rough-hew them as we may." I agree completely with that melancholic gentleman. I have, as you, Honourable judges and members of the Jury know, one other appointment to keep. I am to meet the Princess of Gunung Ledang. And so I pray you will be kind to me, let me move on my journey in that direction, for there at last, where she awaits, I will find peace away from this humdrum existence. I can already hear her call, far in the distance, in that unmistakable melodious voice. In that direction I must soon go. Thank you, your Honours, thank you members of the jury; thank you, lovers of the theatre. It has been an altogether worthy encounter; and here let me rest my case.

Lights dim; everyone rises as the Princess of Gunung Ledang descends from the sky, and performs a solo dance. On the completion of her dance, she rises into the air and disappears. Everyone sits. Lights brighten and the action resumes as before.

JUDGE 1:   This brings us to the end of the trial of our hero. Hang Tuah the Great. It is now your duty, honourable members of the jury, to retire and to deliberate the events you have witnessed, a virtual unfolding of our history, which like all interesting theatre, had moments of comedy, tragedy, excitement as well as pathos. The verdict you will arrive at must bear in mind all the statements made by the defendant, witnesses, as well as the re-enactment of events before your very eyes through this wonderful medium of the theatre. No doubt at street corners, under the glow of street lamps, in amusement parks, in shopping complexes, in coffee-shops and bars, in the classrooms of schools and universities as well as in the chambers of learned men, the subjects will be hotly debated in the manner of all sensational issues. You must not be influenced by these discussions. Remember, not all of them take place in the ideal atmosphere, with a sense of appropriate sobriety and balance. There is thus the inevitable danger of injustice being perpetrated. And when, having taken your time, you have arrived at the verdict, we will, God-willing, gather again to hear it. Meanwhile, good luck and best wishes to all of you, honourable members of the jury. This court now stands adjourned *sine die*. (*Clap of cymbals.*)

BAILIFF: *Bangun!*

Stage lights dim, and fade off. All, including audience stand. The judges leave in the same manner in which they entered at the beginning of the play. Hang Tuah also leaves in the same manner in which he entered in Scene 1, and then the others exit in different directions.

Glossary

Adat	—	Malay customary practice
Ayat	—	A verse or verses from the Holy Quran
Bangsa	—	Race or community
Bangsawan	—	A form of transitional Malay theatre
Bangun	—	To arise, or stand up
Bendahara	—	State Treasurer
Berhantu	—	A ceremony involving raising of spirits
Bhuta	—	Sanskrit word for demon, usually written in Malay as Bota
Bidadari	—	Sanskrit word for nymph
Bomoh	—	Traditional Malay healer or shaman
Dayang	—	A female attendant
Derhaka	—	Disobediance or disloyalty
Dewa	—	Sanskrit word for deity or god
Dewi	—	Sanskrit word for goddess
Dunia Melayu	—	The Malay world in a symbolic manner
Halus	—	Refined, civilized
Hantu	—	Spirit or invisible entity, a generic term
Hara-kiri	—	Japanese word for honorable self-killing
Hikayat	—	Arabic word meaning story, a genre of literature
Hikayat Hang Tuah	—	Malay epic on the life and adventures of Hang Tuah
Ilmu	—	knowledge, usually of a religious or secret variety
Ilmu jahat	—	knowledge usually connected with black magic

105

Kaliyuga	—	the Age of Kali
Kalki	—	In Hinduism, the last incarnation of Vishnu, yet to come
Kathakali	—	A for of traditional dance theatre in Kerala, South India
Kampung	—	A village
Kaput	—	A word suggesting beheading
Kayangan	—	In Malay mythology, the Sky country, home to gods and demons
Keris	—	A short Malay dagger
Kompang	—	A variety of Malay frame-drum beaten by the hand
Kyai	—	A Javanese term of respect; a wise man
Laksmana	—	Commander of the navy
Maghrib	—	The fourth of five Muslim prayers, offered each day at sunset
Mak yong	—	A form of traditional Malay dance-theatre active in Kelantan state
Mek mulong	—	A form of traditional Malay dance theatre active in Kedah state
Menora	—	A form of southern Thai dance theatre also active n northern Malaysia
Nadhaswaram:	—	The south Indian oboe
Pantun	—	A form of Malay poetry written in quatrains
Pawang	—	A traditional Malay healer, same as bomoh
Raja	—	A king of prince
Rakshasa	—	Sanskrit for demon
Rakyat	—	Ordinary citizens
Rubaiyat	—	A form of Arabic and Persian poetry written in quatrains
Sandiwara	—	A form of modern Malay theatre
Sejarah Melayu	—	*The Malay Annals*
Sekolah pondok	—	A village school

Sembah	—	The salutation gesture, same as Indian *anjali* done with palms joined
Sepak raga	—	A traditional game played with a ball of woven rattan
Silat	—	The Malay-Indonesian art of self-defense
Wayang kulit	—	The traditional Malay-Indonesian shadow play

PROFESSOR DATO' DR GHULAM-SARWAR YOUSOF

Personal Information

Professor Dato' Ghulam Sarwar Yousof graduated in English from the University of Malaya (1964), and did a Doctorate in Asian Theatre at the University of Hawaii (1976). He is one of Malaysia's most distinguished scholars of performing arts and one of the world's leading specialists of traditional Southeast Asian theatre.

He was responsible for setting up Malaysia's first Performing Arts programme at the Science University of Malaysia (USM) in Penang in 1970. Dato' Ghulam Sarwar Yousof served at that university as lecturer and Associate Professor. He joined the Cultural Centre, University of Malaya (UM) as Professor in 2002.

Currently he is Senior Academic Fellow in the Department of English Language and Literature, International Islamic University Malaysia, and also Expert/Pakar at the Cultural Centre, University of Malaya, Kuala Lumpur. He is also Director of The Asian Cultural Heritage Centre Berhad, a private research initiative set up by him to promote research in traditional Asian cultures.

Apart from traditional Asian theatre, his major interests include Asian literatures, folklore studies, as well as South—and Southeast Asian cultures, comparative religion, mythology and, Sufism. In ethnographic and folklore studies he has explored Malay-Indonesian mythology and folk literature, Malay concepts of the soul (*semangat*), and *angin* as well as traditional healing processes, and their role in the cases of disease as well as healing.

As a creative writer, he has published poetry, drama as well as short stories. He has also done a translation of Kalidasa's Sanskrit play *Shakuntala* as well as translations of Urdu poetry into English.

Dato' Ghulam-Sarwar Yousof's most outstanding contribution to academia is in traditional Southeast Asian Theatre. In this area he has carved a unique niche for himself, with meticulous field work and research, in some previously unexplored genres, resulting in the most important existing publication, his *Dictionary of Traditional Southeast Asian Theatre*. His vast collection of fieldwork materials and documentation is currently held by the Asian Cultural Heritage Centre Berhad. Among other things, he is currently working on a two-volume anthology of Islamic Literature.

Dato' Ghulam-Sarwar Yousof has held visiting positions as professor at several universities, has lectured in many countries in both Asia and Europe on a broad spectrum of culture-related subjects and on altogether unclassifiable disciplines alike to absolute novices and specialized audiences. He has also given readings of his poetry and short stories as well as organised major poetry events in Kuala Lumpur and Penang in conjunction with UNESCO World Poetry Day. He has been, over the decades, involved in various capacities in numerous cultural organizations, national and international, including the Asia-Europe Foundation as Malaysia's official representative and member of the foundation's Board of Governors.

Academic Awards

East-West Centre Grant for a Doctoral Programme at the Department of Drama and Theatre, University of Hawaii, Honolulu, USA. *September 1972 to September 1976.*

Universiti Sains Malaysia Academic Staff Training Scheme (ASTS) Fellowship for a Doctoral Programme at the Department of Drama and Theatre, University of Hawaii, Honolulu, USA. *September 1972 to September 1977.*

Universiti Sains Malaysia, Penang, Research Grants for Research, Field Work and Documentation of Traditional Malay Theatre Genres. *1978 to 1994.*

Institute of Southeast Asian Studies, Singapore, Research Grant. *June 1983-June 1984.*

Southeast Asian Studies Programme (SEASP), Institute of Southeast Asian Studies, Singapore, teaching and Research Exchange Fellowships Award. *June 1983 to March 1984.*

Southeast Asian Studies Programme (SEASP), Institute of Southeast Asian Studies, Singapore, Cross-Cultural Research and Writing Award. *June 1983 to March 1984.*

Awards of Recognition

Tokoh Maal-Hijrah (Persatuan Melayu Pulau Pinang), 2001.

International Award for Outstanding Contribution for Humanity, Peace, Culture and Education (Forum for Culture and Human Development, Bangladesh), 2001.

Dove Award for Excellence in Poetry awarded (Poetry Day Australia), 2001.

Darjah Setia Pangkuan Negeri (DSPN), which carries the title of Dato' awarded by the Tuan Yang Terutama Yang DiPertua Negeri Pulau Pinang (Governor of Penang), 2008.

Boh Cameronian Lifetime Achievement Award (Kakiseni Malaysia), 2008.

Academic Publications

Articles in Journals

1. **"Revival of an Ancient Tradition: The Mak Yong Dance Theatre of Malaysia"**. *Culture Learning Institute Report* (East West Centre, Honolulu), 4,3 (August 1976), pp4-5, 11&13.
2. **"Barong"** in Bali in *Pesta Pulau Pinang*. Special Publication, Penang, December 1979, pp.9.
3. **"Wayang Wong"** in Bali in *Pesta Pulau Pinang*. Special Publication, Penang, December 1979, pp.10-11.
4. **"Nora Chatri in** Kedah". *Journal of the Malaysian Branch, Royal Asiatic Society*, Vol. IV, Part I (1982), pp.53-61.
5. **"The Play of Shadows: Hindu Elements in the Malay Wayang Kulit Siam"**. *The India Magazine* (New Delhi), Vol.3, No.1 (December 1982), pp.32-39.
6. **"Mak Yong, The Ancient Malay Dance Theatre"**. *Asian Studies* (Manila), Vol.XX (April, August, December 1982), pp.108-121.
7. **"Malaysia-Singapore Drama in English: Themes and Styles"** in Bruce Bennet, Ee Tiang Hong and Ron Sheppard (ed), *The Writer's Sense of the Contemporary: Papers in Southeast Asian and Australian Literature. Nedlands, Western Australia: The Centre for Studies in Australian Literature*, University of Western Australia, 1982, pp.21-25.
8. **"Mak Yong: The Ancient Malay Dance Theatre"**. *Hansa* (Kuala Lumpur), November 1982, pp.8-14.
9. **"Feasting of the Spirits: The Berjamu Ritual Performance in the Kelantanese Wayang Kulit Siam"**. *Kajian Malaysia*, (*Journal of Malaysian Studies*, Penang), 1, 1(June 1982), pp.95-115.
10. **"Buka Panggung: Theatre Consecration Rituals in the Mak Yong Dance Theatre of Kelantan, Malaysia"**. *Tenggara* 16 (1983), pp.55-72.

11. "Ramayana Branch Stories in the Wayang Siam Shadow Play in Malaysia" in K.R. Srinivasa Iyengar (ed). *Asian Variations in Ramayana*. New Delhi: Sahitya Akademi, 1983, pp.296-323.

12. "Traditional Theatre in Southeast Asia". *Performing Arts* (Singapore), No.2 (July 1985), pp.37-49.

13. "Parsi Theatre in Malaysia". *Sangeet Natak* (new Delhi), No. 85-86 (July-December 1986), pp.5-22.

14. "Bangsawan: the Malay Opera". *Tenggara* 20 (1987), pp.3-20.

15. "Thespis Among the Malays" in *Proceedings, International Meeting of the Ancient Greek Drama, Delphi*, 4-21 June 1985. Athens: European Cultural Centre at Delphi, 1987, pp.303-311.

16. "A Previously Unknown Version of the Ramayana from Kedah, Malaysia". In D.P.Sinha and S.Sahai (ed). *Ramayana Traditions and National Cultures Asia*. Lucknow: Directorate of Cultural Affairs and Government of Uttar Pradesh, 1989, pp.131-137.

17. "Tarnishing Gold: The Feudal Hero in Contemporary Malay Drama". In Kirpal Singh (ed). *The Writer's Sense of the Past: Essays on Southeast Asian and Australasian Literature*. Singapore: Singapore National University Press Ltd., 1987, pp.34-45.

18. "The Shadow Play in Southeast Asia: Origins, General Characteristics and Performance Techniques" in *The Arts* (Centre for the Arts, National University of Singapore) Issue No.5, December 1997, pp.11-17.

19. "The Shadow Play in Southeast Asia: The Shadow Play Styles of the Region" in *The Arts* (Centre for the Arts, National University of Singapore) Issue No.6, April 1998, pp.19-24.

20. "The Malay-Indonesian Shadow Play as a Manifestation of Cultural Continuities" in *Tirai Panggung*. Jurnal Seni Persembahan, Pusat Kebudayaan, Universiti Malaya, Jilid 5, (2002), ms 1-16.

21. **"The Continuing Significance of Epics and their Manifestations in the Arts"** in Ghulam-Sarwar Yousof (ed). *Reflections on Asian-European Epics.* Singapore: Asia-Europe Foundation, 2004, pp.1-11.

22. **"The Ramayana and the Mahabharata as Sources of Repertoire in Traditional Southeast Asian Theatre"** in Ghulam-Sarwar Yousof (ed). *Reflections on Asian-European Epics.* Singapore: Asia-Europe Foundation, 2004. pp.302-329.

23. **"Religious and Spiritual Values in Kalidasa's Shakuntala"** in *Katha*: The Official Journal of the Centre for Civilisational Dialogue, University of Malaya, Kuala Lumpur, Inaugural Issue, 2005. pp.21-39.

24. **"Search for Traditional Theatre in Southeast Asia: A Personal Odyssey"** in Edwin Thumboo (ed). *Perceiving Other Worlds.* Singapore: Intl Specialized Book Service Inc. pp.100-110.

25. **"The Shadow Play as a Continuing, Changing Tradition"** in Faridah Noor Mohd Noor (Editor). *Dimensions of the Shadow Play in Malay Civilisation.* Kuala Lumpur: Centre for Civilisational Dialogue, University of Malaya, 2006, pp.1-26.

26. **Islamic Elements in Traditional Indonesian and Malay Theatre**. *Kajian Malaysia*, Journal of the School of Humanities, Universiti Sains Malaysia Vol 28, No. 1 (2010), 83-101.

27. **"Tradition and Sundering with Tradition: Mak yong from Traditional to Tinsel** Theatre and Beyond.". *Tirai Panggung*, Performing Arts Journal, Cultural Centre, University of Malaya, vol 10 (2010), 45-61.

28. **"The Story of the Conch Shell Prince in Traditional Malay Theatre"** in *SSEASR Journal*, India, vol 5 (2011), 21-32.

International Conferences/ Seminar Papers

1. **"Recent Malaysian-Singapore Drama in English: Problems & Prospects"**. *New Drama in English Conference*, Canberra, Australia, 1979.
2. **"Ramayana Branch Stories in the Wayang Siam Shadow Play of Malaysia"**. *International Seminar on Variations in ramayana: Their cultural, Social and Anthropological Significance*. New Delhi, 1981.
3. **"A Separate Truth: Themes and Styles in Contemporary Malaysian-Singapore English Language Drama"**. *Southeast Asian and Australian Literature Seminar*, University of Western Australia, Nedlands, Perth, Western Australia, 1982.
4. **"The Ritual Context of Traditional Malay Theatre"**. *Asian Theatre Festival and Conference*, Manila, 1983.
5. **"Tarnishing Gold: The feudal Hero in Modern Malay Drama"**. *Southeast Asian and Australian Literature Seminar*, Singapore, 1984.
6. **"Thespis Among the Malays"**. *International Meeting of Ancient Greek Drama*. Delphi, Greece, 1985.
7. **"Preservation of Traditional Malay Theatre, with special reference to Bangsawan"**. *ASEAN Interaction, Australian and New Zealand Association of Arts and Sciences (ANZAAS) Festival of Science*, Melbourne, 1985.
8. **"Preliminary Proposal for the Establishment of Community Resource Centres"**. *9th National Conference of the Musicological Society of Australia,* Monash University, Melbourne, 1985.
9. **"Sita Dewi Forsworn: An Uttarakanda Episode in the Malay Wayang Kulit Siam"**. *2nd International Seminar Ramayana Conference*, Bangkok, 1986.
10. **"A Previously Unknown Version of the Ramayana from Kedah, Malaysia"**. *International Seminar on Ramayana Traditions and National Cultures in Asia*. Lucknow, India, 1986.

11. "The Malay-Indonesian Shadow Play as a Manifestation of Cultural Continuities". *Seminar on Tradition: A Continual Renewal.* New Delhi, 1987.
12. "Malaysian and Southeast Asian Theatre". *Festival of Hungry Ghosts Celebration.* Adelaide, 1988.
13. "Search for Traditional Theatre in Southeast Asia: A Personal Odyssey". *Seminar on Perceiving Other Cultures,* National University of Singapore, 1989.
14. "Indigenous Mythology and Traditional Malay Theatre". *International Seminar on Southeast Asian Traditional Performing Arts: the State of the Art,* Universiti Sains Malaysia, 1992.
15. "The Dewa Muda Story: its Significance in Mak Yong and Main Puteri Performances—Spiritual and Non-Spiritual". *Mak Yong Seminar,* Universiti Sains Malaysia, 1995.
16. "On the Possible Origins of the Malay Shadow Play and its Relationship with the Shadow Plays of Southeast Asia". *SEMEO-SPAFA Symposium on History of the Performing Arts in Southeast Asia.* Kuala Lumpur, 1997.
17. "Images of Europe in Asia" *Conference on Images of Asia in Europe and Images of Europe in Asia.* Asia-Europe Foundation, Danish Cultural Centre, Copenhagen, 1999.
18. "Preservation of Traditional Heritage: Some Challenges". Anst
19. "The Continuing Significance of Epics and their Manifestations in the Arts" *International Seminar on Asian-European Epics.* University of Malaya, 2002.
20. "The Ramayana and the Mahabharata as Sources of Repertoire in Traditional Southeast Asian Theatre". *International Seminar on Asian-European Epics.* University of Malaya, 2002.
21. "Reflections on Poetry and the Self". *Writer's Talk.* National University of Singapore. 2004.
22. "The Malay Shadow Play as a Continuing but Changing Tradition" *International Shadow Play Conference.* Centre for

Civilisational Dialogue University of Malaya & Museum of Asian Art University of Malaya. Kuala Lumpur, 2004.

23. **"Ruminations on the Origins and Functions of the Mak Yong Dance Theatre**" *International Seminar on Asian Theatre: Tradition, Modernity and Innovation in Asian Theatre,* University of Malaya, 2004.

24. **"Current State of Malaysian Puppetry**". *Puppets-Facing the Interior-Memory, Recovery and Transposition: the Asian Experience.* UNESCO-APPAN Puppetry Symposium and Festival. Bangkok, 2004.

25. **"Malaysian Shadow Play**" *Performance Studies International: PSI 10: Performance State Interrogate.* Singapore Management Univeristy, 2004.

26. **"The 1969 Crisis as Turning Point: the Search for a Malaysian Literary Identity**". *11th Biennial Symposium on the Literatures and Cultures of the Asia-Pacific Region/ Literatures in Englishes and Their Centres: perceiving from the Inside.* National University of Singapore. 2005.

27. **"From Kampung to Istana Budaya: transformation of Mak Yong: An Ancient Form of Malay Theatre**". *International Traditional Theatre Fesival: The Moment of Insight.* National Arts Academy, Kuala Lumpur, 2006.

28. **"The Story of the Golden Shell Prince in Traditional Malay Theatre**". *2nd SSEASR Conference on Syncretism in South and Southeast Asia: Adoption and Adaptation.* Bangkok, 2007.

29. **"Tradition and Sundering with Tradition: Mak Yong from Traditional to Tinsel Theatre and Beyond**". *PACIA 08, International Conference on Performing Arts as Creative Industries in Asia.* Cultural Centre, University of Malaya, Kuala Lumpur, 2008.

30. **"Indigenous Beliefs, Mythology and Folk Islam: The Malaysian Context, with Special Reference to Traditional Malay Theatre**". *International Folklore Conference.* Department of Oriya, Visva-Bharati University, in collaboration with Central Institute of Indian

Languages, Mysore, Shantineketan, India, 18-20 February 2008.

31. **"Ramayana in Southeast Asian Performing Arts".** *Ramayana: Ramkatha: Ankan, Manchan aur Vachan.* Indira Gandhi National Centre for the Arts, New Delhi, India, March 12-20 2008.

32. **"Islamic Elements in Traditional Southeast Asian Theatre"** *Colours of Indian Islamic Culture: Together with Faith" (Hind Islami Tahzeeb ke Rang: Aqeedat ke Sang).* Indira Gandhi National Centre for the Arts, New Delhi, India, 1-8 April 2008.

33. "Mak yong and the Notion of Malayness". Paper presented at **Imagined Communities Revisited: Identity, Nationalism and Globalisation in Asia-Pacific Literatures and Cultures** Conference, Department of English, International Islamic University Malaysia, Kuala Lumpur, November 20-23 2009.

34. "Ramayana in Southeast Asian Traditional Theatre Performances: Adaptation and Localization" Paper submitted for presentation at the International Conference **Ramayana: Retelling, Representation and Reinterpretation in Asia.** Asian Civilisations Museum, Singapore July 17-1 2010.

35. **The Mak yong Dance Theatre as Spiritual Heritage: Some Insights.**" Keynote Paper presented at the SPAAFA International Seminar on *The Mak Yong Spiritual Dance Heritage: Seminar and Performances* held in September 2011.

36. **Puppetry as a Manifestation of Cultural Traditions of a Nation".** Paper presented at the *Union Internationales de la Marionettes (UNIMA International Seminar,* October 17-18 2011, at SENAWANGI Jakarta, Indonesia.

37. **"South Asian Puppetry: Convergences and Divergences.**" Keynote Paper presented at the *International Seminar of ASEAN Puppetry: Tradition and Modernity* organized by the ASEAN Puppetry Association (APA) and

the University of Malaya Cultural Centre, University of Malaya, Kuala Lumpur, Malaysia, November 2-3 2011.

Articles in Magazines

1. **"Bangsawan, the People's Opera"**. *Pulau Pinang*, Vol.1 (Jan-Feb 1989), pp.9-12
2. **"Rites of Ramadan"**. *Pulau Pinang*, Vol.2 (March-April 1989), pp.29-30
3. **"Lasting Charisma"**. *Pulau Pinang*, Vol.2 (March-April 1989), pp.31-35.
4. **"Hari Raya Haji"**. *Pulau Pinang*, Vol.3 (May-June 1989), pp.32-34.
5. **"The Malay Performing Arts of Penang"**. *Penang Past & Present*, Vol.7 (April 2000), pp.7-18.

Chapters in Books

1. **"Traditional Teater Melayu; Satu Pengenalan"**. Bab 2 *Apresiasi Seni Teater Malaysia*. (ed. Said Halim Said Nong). Kuala Lumpur, Pusat Kebudayaan Universiti Malaya, 2009, ms 27-50.
2. **"Ramayana in the Malaysian Wayang Kulit Siam"** Chapter in *Ramayana in Focus: Visual and Performing Arts of Asia*. (Ed, Gauri Parimoo Krishnan) pp. 134-143. Singapore: Asian Civilizations Museum, 2010.
3. **"Mak Yong and the Notion of Malayness."** Nor Faridah Abdul and Mohammad A. Quayum, eds. *Imagined Communities Revisited: Critical Essays on Asia-Pacific Literatures and Cultures*. Kuala Lumpur: IIUM Press, 2011. 148-56.
4. **"The Almost Enforced Mingling of Cultures: Anthony Burgess' Depiction of Races and Race Relations in Pre-Independence Malaya."** Chapter 2 in Md Mahmudul

Hasan (Ed.) *Crossing Boundaries: Musings on Language, Literature and Culture.* Kuala Lumpur: International University of Malaya Press, 2012, pp. 17-29.

5. **"Mirza Ghalib as a Mystical Poet: Introducing Two Urdu Ghazals.**" Chapter 6 in Md Mahmudul Hasan (Ed.) *Crossing Boundaries: Musings on Language, Literature and Culture.* Kuala Lumpur: International University of Malaya Press, 2012, pp. 61-70.

6. **"The South Asian Impact upon Traditional Malay Theatre."** Chapter 7 in Arvind Sharma and Madhu Khanna(Ed) *Asian Perspectives on the World's Religions after September 11.* Santa Barbara, California: Praeger, 2013, pp. 89-107.

Books

1. **Ceremonial and Decorative Crafts of Penang.** Penang: State Museum, 1986.
2. **Bibliography of Traditional Theatre in Southeast Asia.** Singapore: Institute of Southeast Asian Studies, 1991.
3. **Panggung Semar: Aspects of Traditional Malay Theatre.** Kuala Lumpur: Tempo Publishing (M) Sdn. Bhd., 1992.
4. **Dictionary of Traditional Southeast Asian Theatre.** Kuala Lumpur: Oxford University Press, 1994.
5. **Angin Wayang: Biography of a Master Puppeteer.** Kuala Lumpur: Ministry of Culture, Arts and Tourism, 1997.
6. **Angin Wayang: Biografi Seorang Dalang yang unggul.** Kuala Lumpur: Ministry of Culture, Arts and Tourism, 1997.
7. **The Malay Shadow Play: An Introduction.** Penang: the Asian Centre, 1997.
8. **Panggung Inu: Aspects of Traditional Malay Theatre.** Singapore: National University of Singapore Cultural centre, 2004.

9. **Heritage of ASEAN Puppetry.** Jakarta: Sena Wangi, 2013.
10. **Issues in Traditional Malaysian Culture.** Singapore: Trafford Publishing, 2013.

Books—Compilation of Poems

1. **Encounters with Realities: Poems 1962-2012**. Kuala Lumpur: Asian Cultural Centre. 2013.

Edited Volumes

1. **Reflections on Asian-European Epics**. (Edited by Ghulam-Sarwar Yousof). Singapore: Editions Didier Millet, Archipelago Press, 2004.
2. **Encyclopedia of Malaysia. Vol 8, Performing Arts**. Editor: Ghulam-Sarwar Yousof. Singapore: Archipelago Press. Editions Didier Millet, 2004 13.
3. Nakayama, Machiko. **500 Years of Ikebana. (Editor** Ghulam-Sarwar Yousof Kuala Lumpur: Asian Cultural Heritage Centre Bhd, 2013

Encyclopedia Entries

Entries in **Encyclopedia of Malaysia, Vol 8, Performing Arts**. Editor: Ghulam-Sarwar Yousof. Singapore: Archipelago Press. Editions Didier Millet, 2004.

* Introduction pp 6-7
* Origins and History of Performing Arts in Malaysia pp10-11
* Belief Systems of Traditional Theatre pp12-13
* Story-telling and Elementary Theatre pp14

- Story-telling and Solo Theatre pp15
- Puppet Theatre pp22-23
- Malay Shadow Theatre in Southeast Asia pp24-25
- Wayang Kulit Siam: the Kelantan Shadow Play pp26-27
- Wayang Kulit Siam: the Dalang, his Puppets and Stories pp28-29
- Wayang Kulit Gedek, Melayu and Purwa pp30-31
- Mak Yong: Ancient Folk Theatre pp38-39
- Operatic Genres pp52-53
- Theatre as Ritual, Ritual as Theatre pp60-61
- Healing Performance pp62-63
- Mak Yong as Ritual pp64-65
- Wayang Kulit Siam as Ritual pp66-67
- Court Patronage of the Performing Arts pp88-89
- Mak Yong's Court Sojourn pp94-95
- Islam and the Performing Arts pp96-97
- Middle Eastern Influences in Traditional Malay Theatre pp98-99
- Malay Vocal Music pp100-101
- Boria pp104
- Contemporary Performing Arts pp106-107
- Arts Organizations and their Contributions pp124-125
- Teaching and Research in the Performing Arts pp126-127
- Malay Films and Television Dramas pp128-129

Entries in **Encyclopedia of Malaysia, Vol 12, Peoples and Traditions**. Editor: Hood Salleh. Singapore: Archipelago press, Editions Didier Millet, 2006.

- Malay Traditions (co-author with Wan Hashim Wan The) pp32-33
- Cross Cultural Influences pp134-135
- Common Identity and Cultural Fusion pp136-137
- Malaysia and World Culture pp 138-139

Entries in **Encyclopedia of Malaysia, Vol 14, Crafts and Visual Arts**. Editor: Syed Ahmad Jamal. Singapore: Archipelago Press, Editions Didier Millet, 2007.

- Recreational and Ceremonial Crafts pp94-95
- Puppetry pp96-97
- Malay Kites and Tops pp98-99
- Chinese and Indian Religious Art and Crafts pp102-102

Entries in **Encyclopedia of Malaysia, Vol 15. Sports and Recreation**. Editor: Ahmad Sarji Abdul Hamid. Singapore: Archipelago Press, Editions Didier Millet, 2008.

- Traditional Games and Pastimes pp 14
- Top Spinning pp16
- Kite Flying pp18

Monographs

1. **Muslim Festivals: Essence and Observance**. Islamic Information Centre, Malayan Pakistani League, Penang, 1989.
2. **Traditional Theatre in Southeast Asia: An Introduction**. Penang: Pusat Seni, Universiti Sains Malaysia, 1993. Monographs on Southeast Asian Cultures series.
3. **Mak Yong Theatre of Kelantan, Malaysia: An Introduction.** Kuala Lumpur: The Asian Cultural Heritage Centre Berhad, 2011.

LITERARY PUBLICATIONS

1. **Ghulam-Sarwar Yousof.** *Perfumed Memories.* Singapore: Graham Brash Pte Ltd., 1982. Collection of Poems

2. **Ghulam-Sarwar Yousof**. *Halfway Road, Penang*. Penang. Teks Publishing Company, (1982). Reprinted by The Asian Cultural Heritage Centre, Penang, 2002. (Drama text).
3. **Ghulam-Sarwar Yousof** (comp). *Mirror of a Hundred Hue*s. Penang: The Asian Cultural Heritage Centre, 2001. (A Miscellany)
4. **Ghulam-Sarwar Yousof**. *Songs for Shooting Stars: Mystical Verse*. Pittsburgh, PA 15222, USA: Lauriat Press, 2011. (Collection of Poems.)
5. **Ghulam-Sarwar Yousof**. *Transient Moments*. Kuala Lumpur: The Asian Centre, 2012. (Selected Poems)

Poems in Anthologies

1. Thumboo, Edwin (ed). *The Second Tongue: An Anthology of Poetry from Malaysia and Singapore*. Singapore: Heinemann, 1976.
2. Hashmi, Alamgir (ed). *The Worlds of Muslim Imagination*. Islamabad: Gulmohar, 1986.
3. Malachi, Edwin (ed). *Insight: Malaysian Poems*. Petaling Jaya: Maya Press, 2003.
4. Maya Press. *The Spirit of the Keris*. Petaling Jaya: Maya Press, 2003.
5. Rosli Talif and Noritah Omar (ed). *Petals of Hibiscus: A Representative Anthology of Malaysian Literature in English*. Petaling Jaya: Pearsons Malaysia Sdn Bhd, 2003.
6. Thumboo, Edwin (ed). *& Words: Poems Singapore and Beyond*. Singapore: Ethos Books, 2010.

Random Poems Published

Random poems have appeared in the following journals:

- *Lidra* (Kuala Lumpur)

- *Mele* (Honolulu)
- *Impulse* (Honolulu)
- *Pacific Quarterly* (Hamilton, New Zealand)
- *Dewan Sastera* (Kuala Lumpur)
- *Solidarity* (Manila)

Short Stories

"Lottery Ticket", "Birthday", "Tok Dalang" and "Dewi Ratnasari" in *Mirror of a Hundred Hues: A Miscellany.* Penang: The Asian Centre, 2001.

TRANSLATIONS/ADAPTATIONS

- The Mak Yong play "Raja Tangkai Hati" translated from Malay into English and adapted for a production at the Kennedy Theatre, University of Hawaii, 1973.
- Kalidasa' "Shakuntala", translated for a production done in Kuala Lumpur by the Temple of Fine Arts, Kuala Lumpur, 1982.
- Sophocles' "Oedipus Rex". Rewritten in modern English and adapted, 1987.

CONSULTANCY

Proclamation of Mak Yong Theatre as Intangible Cultural Heritage by UNESCO IN 2005
On behalf of the Malaysian Ministry of Culture, Arts and Heritage, Ghulam-Sarwar Yousof was responsible for the preparation to nominate Mak Yong, the ancient traditional Malay dance theatre form for consideration as an item of The Oral and Intangible Heritage of Humanity. Mak Yong received the recognition in November 2005.

International Appointments

- *Theatre Consultant* for Mindanao State University—Iligan Institute of Technology, Iligan City, Philippines, 1984
- *Governor for Malaysia*, Asia-Europe Foundation (Malaysian representative on the Board of Governors of this Foundation which has 26 members-25 countries from Asia and Europe as well as the European Union), 1999-2005
- *Member, Regional Review Committee*, Asian Scholarship Foundation (Funded by Ford Foundation in Bangkok) 2004-2006
- *Founding Committee Member*, ASEAN Puppetry Association (Established in Jakarta) 2006-Present.
- *Presidium Chairman*, ASEAN Puppetry Association, 2011 to present.

Local Appointments

- *Director of Research*, Yayasan Seni, Kuala Lumpur, Malaysia. 1990-1
- *Consultant on Cultural Traditions*, Socio-Economic and Environmental Research Institute, Penang. 2000-1
- *Consultant on Culture*, Jawatankuasa Bidang Teras, Jabatan Perdana Menteri (Priime Minister's Department) Penang. 2001
- *Consultant*, Nomination of the Mak Yong Dance Theatre form to UNESCO to be considered as an item of the Oral and Intangible Heritage of Mankind. 2004-5.
- *Member* Malaysian Branch of the Royal Asiatic Society. 2005-current
- *Member*, Penang Heritage Advisory Committee, 2009-current.

- Academic Advisor, English Department, TAR University College, Kuala Lumpur, 2011-current.
- Expert/Pakar, Cultural Centre, University of Malaya, Kuala Lumpur, 2010 to current.

Email add: gsyousof@um.edu.my; gsyousof@iium.edu.my; gsyousof@hotmail.com

September 2013